SHADOW'S HOAX

SHADOW ISLAND SERIES: BOOK TWELVE

MARY STONE
LORI RHODES

Copyright © 2023 by Mary Stone Publishing

All rights reserved.

No part of this book may be reproduced in any form or by any electronic or mechanical means, including information storage and retrieval systems, without written permission from the author, except for the use of brief quotations in a book review.

❦ Created with Vellum

This book is dedicated to all New Year's resolution-makers. May your willpower be stronger than the temptation of a midnight snack, and your determination as steadfast as a secret password. Here's to a year where 'I'll start on Monday' becomes reality. Happy New Year, and good luck with those resolutions – if you're like me, you'll need it!

DESCRIPTION

Every clue is a countdown.

A typical morning at Sandpiper Bank turns into chaos when an armed man in a clown costume storms in, shattering the calm. He trashes the lobby and executes the bank manager, even after securing the money, hinting at a motive beyond mere robbery.

Maybe money isn't the root of all evil, after all.

Puzzled by the senseless violence, Sheriff Rebecca West is drawn into a labyrinth of mystery and danger as the bank's connections to the Yacht Club are revealed. The arrival of the FBI, led by Rebecca's former instructor, offers a mix of relief and renewed tension. Together, they uncover a string of unsettling links to Shadow Island, each discovery more perplexing than the last.

As Rebecca inches ever closer to the sinister truths lurking within the Yacht Club, she finds herself plunged into treacherous waters. In this world of duplicity and danger, trust is a rare commodity, and the stakes skyrocket beyond the confines of the law.

Rebecca isn't just chasing clues anymore...she's fighting to stay afloat in a maelstrom of deceit. But as she delves deeper, she finds herself in the deep end...and sinking fast.

From the intriguing beginning to the electrifying conclusion, Shadow's Hoax—the twelfth book in the Shadow Island series by Mary Stone and Lori Rhodes—plays out like a chess match. But in this deadly game, who is the pawn?

1

"Hurry up, ladies. It's nearly time to open."

Arthur Carson shook his keys toward the three teller windows where his staff sorted and stocked their tills. The lobby of the Sandpiper Bank was spotless, as usual. Every weekend, the cleaning service polished the worn tiles and old-fashioned brass fixtures at each teller window.

For the type of clientele they attracted, everything had to be perfect.

"No one's ever here when we open on Mondays." Stephanie, his youngest teller at only eighteen, always teased him about his by-the-book attitude. According to her, such fussiness contrasted with island living. "We've got plenty of time to get ready."

Arthur rested one hand on the push bar of the front door. Muscle memory guided the key into the lock as he called over his shoulder. "Never say never. As soon as you do, the universe will do its damnedest to prove you wrong." He quarter-turned the dead bolt to the right, opening the door. "Besides, we all know—"

As the bank door swung open, a rough hand reached through and shoved him backward.

Arthur landed on his back with enough force that he slid a few feet, his elbow taking the brunt of the impact. It was only by luck that his head landed on the large rug with the Sandpiper logo instead of the tile floor.

Someone muscled through the doorway. "Stop what you're doing and put your hands up!"

Shock coursed through Arthur like electricity. *A robbery? Really?*

Adrenaline surged through him when the dead bolt slammed into place.

My keys!

He stared at his empty right hand. Then lifted his gaze to the door.

A clown blocked his view. He blinked rapidly, certain he was hallucinating.

How hard did I hit my head?

A Halloween-style rubber mask grinned at him with a wide, rounded, synthetic smile. The clown wore stereotypically frizzy red hair and sported a bulbous red nose. The rest of the costume consisted of striped, oversize clothes with multicolor pom-poms trailing down the front. The chucklehead standing over him could have passed as any standard-issue clown, if not for the ominous backpack slung over his shoulder.

The clown shoved Arthur's keys into a pocket of the padded costume. But one of the smaller keys hooked on the loose material, leaving it exposed.

Arthur stared at the shoes and realized they were covered in big blue elasticized booties. Like the kind hospital staff wore for sanitary purposes.

The clown stepped forward, the glint of black steel materializing in his gloved hand. Arthur's bowels nearly loosened as he faced his worst fear…the dark barrel of a handgun leveled at his face.

Behind him, screams of shock and panic from his three tellers punctuated the bank's lobby.

"Shut up and do as I say, or I'll put a bullet in his brain!" The command came from behind Chucklehead's unmoving rubber lips.

Without taking his eyes off the macabre maniac, Arthur called to his staff, trying to reassure them. "Do as he says. Remember your training. Don't resist. Hand over the money and follow his instructions."

As the robber stepped over him, Arthur recoiled, covering his head with his hands. A thin *splat* seized his attention, and he glanced up in time to watch a stack of brochures slide across the floor like a glossy wave. Their plastic stand followed, clattering on top of them. In the midst of the commotion, the coffee pot hit the tile, shattering glass and lukewarm Arabica across the strewn brochures.

"Listen up." The clown looked at a piece of paper before stuffing it deep inside his costume. "Empty your tills or your manager's going to die!" Chucklehead's mask faced the three tellers, who'd stopped screaming and were standing with their hands trembling above their heads. "Do you want me to kill him?"

Arthur remained frozen in place as the gun once again pointed at his head. The clown picked up a little stand for business cards from one of the tables in the lobby and slung it across the room.

"Because I will. I have specific instructions that we all need to follow. If you touch the silent alarm, I will shoot him. And I won't stop shooting until there's no one left to call for help."

Instructions. Was this guy so inexperienced he needed someone to tell him how to rob a bank? Had those been crib notes he'd stuffed into his getup?

As threats went, it was straightforward and easy to understand. All three bank tellers stood motionless. Arthur remained on his back, craning his neck so he could keep an eye on the cheerful mask of the criminal terrorizing his three employees.

"Take all the money out of your tills and put it in bags. Do it now. Fast. And don't put any of those dye packs in. I'll see them, and you don't want to give me a reason to get angry while I'm holding a loaded gun."

The tone of Chucklehead's voice remained flat and hard. He walked over to a desk, picked up one of the chairs, and threw it at the cardboard stand for the bank's new home equity program.

As he circled the area, Chucklehead managed to keep his gun pointed at Arthur's head the whole time.

"Do what he said. Give him all the cash, ladies." Arthur twisted around to keep the man in sight. He was too far away to interfere with the clown, and besides, the whole staff had been trained on how to respond to robbers. While this was Arthur's first time putting that training into practice, he knew the main directive. No heroics.

As a cardboard promotional sign for the bank's certificate of deposit rate sailed over the service window, the tellers screamed again.

Jen, the most senior of the tellers, gave a shaky nod to Arthur before heading to her till. That was when Stephanie and Karen regained control of themselves enough to follow Jen's lead.

"Don't you move, man. There's plenty of faces in here that wouldn't look so good with a bullet in them." He continued to sow chaos, moving, throwing, and scattering anything he could shove or throw with one hand.

Arthur noted the gap between the mask and the costume. White makeup covered the scant amount of skin around the clown's eyes. He glanced down, but the clown's wrist was also concealed.

Every time something new crashed into a wall or shattered on the floor, the women behind the counter flinched. Chucklehead's rubber mask hid any feelings he might've had toward their reactions.

Arthur felt helpless and embarrassed as he lay on the floor, useless. He needed to de-escalate the robber's chaotic behavior before someone got shot. "There's no need to do this. We'll give you what you want, and then you can go. It's just money. No one wants to risk their life for it."

The clown stopped his rampage, and Arthur was terrified his words might have invited more danger.

With a deliberate movement that sliced through the tense quiet, the clown pivoted the gun away from Arthur. As the barrel targeted Jen, who stood mere feet away, her face drained of color. "You know, man, it's that kind of smart thinking that will make this so much easier. Hand over the bags."

There was a moment where everyone was paralyzed with fear.

"Hand over the bags!" The command erupted again, more ferocious this time. His rubber-soled slippers squeaked against the floor as he whirled and redirected the gun at Arthur. Chucklehead strode over and grabbed him by the collar. "Or this man's brains will be the next thing to decorate these tiles!"

"Okay. Okay! Here!" Jen tossed her bag onto the counter. She then hurried over to the others and added their bags to make a pile at her window. "That's it. That's everything we have. You can let him go. Just take the money and go."

The clown pulled Arthur's shirt tight across his throat,

forcing him up onto his knees just to relieve the pressure. "I can let him go, but I won't. He's going to stay right here next to me while you all come out from behind there. And keep your hands up where I can see them."

Silently, the three women walked to the end of the teller counter, lifted the swing door shelf, and opened the half door. Karen was shaking so hard that when her foot landed on one of the brochures, she nearly went sprawling. Arthur's heart broke for his friend and colleague. It was his responsibility to comfort and protect the three women.

But he was useless.

"That's good. Now line up in front of your boss, facing the other way. And put your hands behind your backs." The masked man stepped around Arthur. "Boss man, you can stand up now. No funny business, or the executions begin."

Arthur, careful to keep his hands raised, struggled to his feet. From behind him came the sound of a zipper being pulled shut, and his mind raced to picture what the robber was doing. He realized Chucklehead must be retrieving something from his backpack.

"Now we walk these nice ladies to the bathroom." The barrel of the gun hit the back of Arthur's head hard enough to make him stumble forward. "Move."

In the back corner of the lobby was a single-use commode, for the employees more than visitors. Even customers who'd been coming in for most of their lives were unaware of the bank's facilities. Which made Arthur wonder how this man knew about it. Because of the clown costume, visually identifying the man was impossible. Nothing in his movements triggered a memory.

But then again, Arthur was so scared, his mouth tasted like dirty pennies.

The bank wasn't large, so they reached the unmarked door in only a few strides. "Inside. Move it. And keep quiet.

Trust me, you don't want me to come back here. Lay face down on the floor, hands behind your backs."

Shoving his terror down, Arthur tried his best to comfort his tellers. "It'll be okay. You're all being very brave. We're going to get through this."

The four of them would be incredibly cramped packed into such a small room. He'd already made up his mind to position himself closest to the door. Though he wasn't a large man by any means, he could serve as a barrier between the robber and the women who looked up to him. At least it would be something.

It's almost over. If I break, they'll be even more scared. I have to be strong for them. Oh, God, who's going to call Mom every Sunday and on her birthday if I die today? I'm the only family she has left.

"Tape their hands behind their backs. Palms together." Arthur perceived a roll of duct tape bumping against his shoulder even as the cold metal of the gun remained pressed against the back of his head. "And don't try anything funny."

With shaky hands, Arthur took the tape and bound the three women as they whimpered. He started with Stephanie, who was farthest from the door, lying with her feet by the toilet. Next was Karen, who was pressed up against Stephanie's side. Finally, he bound Jen's hands. She was positioned with her head under the sink near the door.

His stomach was sour from violating his employees. Tears streamed down Stephanie's and Karen's faces as they kept glancing over their shoulders at him. Jen had her forehead pressed to the bathroom tile floor, and she was shaking. They were helpless now, and it was all because of him.

Arthur lifted his foot to squeeze in next to Jen by the door, but a hand on his collar yanked him back. Caught off balance, mentally and physically, Arthur fell backward, landing on his hip and elbow—the same one he'd smacked earlier. At fifty-one, he wasn't sure how many more hits his elbow could take without breaking.

"I didn't tell you to go in there. Get up." Chucklehead addressed Arthur's bound tellers. "Ladies, if you so much as crack this door open, I'll blow his brains out. If you know what's good for you and your boss man, you'll stay inside until I'm long gone."

The robber closed the bathroom door and turned. Arthur struggled to his feet as Chucklehead shoved him toward the short hallway that led to his office, the electrical room, and the back door. His mind tried to piece together what the robber could want from this area of the building. "There's no mon—"

"I have all the money I want. It's time for something else." They reached Arthur's office, where he was shoved inside. Losing his footing, he collapsed on the floor in front of his desk, minimally grateful he hadn't landed on his elbow yet again. His breathing was so hard and noisy, he almost missed the robber's next words.

"You need to transfer all the money out of these accounts and send it to the account I have written down here. Get up and start typing."

A folded piece of paper landed on the floor in front of him. Arthur picked it up. As soon as he saw the first account, a chill ran through him. His labored breathing was forgotten as he recognized the numbers on that list.

"No."

A white cotton fist slammed into his cheek, knocking his teeth painfully together as his jaw bounced off the floor. "You'll do it. And you'll forget you ever did it. Hell, you're going to forget I ever asked you to do this. And you're going to forget to add this transaction to the list when you're served with that warrant."

"I won't." His eyebrows furrowed as he pushed himself up

and back onto his knees. He scowled at the monster standing over him. Now he understood how Chucklehead knew his way around the bank. The Yacht Club was behind this. They were calling the shots.

Chucklehead was no longer a clown in Arthur's eyes. Nor was he a robber. He was algae. "You can tell your masters in the Yacht Club I will *never* help them with any of their illegal dealings. It's bad enough that I have to house their dirty money. I'm more than happy to help law enforcement—"

A blue streak slammed into his chest as the clown's booted foot connected with its target, sending Arthur onto his back. The air rushed from his lungs and pain sliced through his sternum, but he was no longer filled with fear. Anger took over, masking the pain of what he suspected was a broken rib or two.

"If you know the Yacht Club, then you know that 'no' is not an option. These guys make much better friends than enemies. Trust me." The goon's foot pressed harder, compressing Arthur's chest.

Arthur lifted his head from the worn tile floor of his office, not noticing the blood that frothed around his lips as the blood from his mouth mixed with his saliva. He looked up into the barrel of Chucklehead's gun. "No."

The eyes behind the clown mask widened, showing their brown color.

He tried to reason with the madman. "No one else in this bank can do what your masters want. Only I have the right passwords, and I refuse. The Aqua Mafia doesn't have friends. They have slaves, they have enemies, and they have victims. Which do you want to be?"

For a moment, the goon seemed confused by the nickname-gone-viral the islanders had taken to using for the entitled thugs who thought they owned everything and everyone. Chucklehead scanned the room before fixing his gaze back on Arthur. "Just do it! Money isn't worth your life!"

"Life is worth more than money. Which is why I will never do what they want. Kill me if you have to. I will never help you or them."

A gloved fist once again smashed into Arthur's mouth.

Arthur rolled from the blow. He was beyond feeling pain now. It didn't matter. A kick to the chest, and then another, slid him backward. Stars blossomed as more jabbing pain erupted in his sternum before he collided with the heavy wood of his desk. He gritted his teeth as a heavy heel stomped his side.

Through the blinding pain radiating through his chest and jaw, Arthur recalled the black plastic button mounted on the side of his desk. It blended in with the dark wood. A hidden alarm.

A sharp blow hit his kidney directly. Crying out, he seized the opportunity to throw himself forward, flinging his arm under the overhanging desktop. Hoping his erratic movement was believable, he slapped his hand against the plastic button. It depressed and stayed in. The silent alarm was enabled. Help was on the way.

"This is your last chance!"

Through the haze of his pain, Arthur detected fear and nervousness in the clown towering over him. He rolled away from the desk to face his attacker.

As he'd done in the lobby, the man in the clown suit was scattering anything he could find across Arthur's floor. There was a desperate energy in his movements.

It made Arthur smile.

The Aqua Mafia hadn't expected him to say no and stick to it. But there was nothing in this world that would convince him to do their bidding. Chucklehead was so busy ransacking the office that he never noticed when Arthur's keys fell out of his pocket. Arthur rolled over with a moan, snatched them, and tucked them into his inner jacket pocket.

The clown spun around, jerking as he looked down at Arthur's bloody, smiling face. "Just move the money, man. Give them what they want so I don't have to do this."

It hit Arthur then. The man didn't want to kill him. Good. Arthur didn't want to die. He tried to sit up, but his muscles weren't working right, and it was hard to talk.

As he worked his jaw, something cracked loose and hit his tongue. He spat the sharp object—a tooth—onto the ground under his desk. "Each of us has to make tough choices in life. I've made mine. I won't help men who pay other men to do things like this. Now you have a choice to make."

Resignation filled the eyes of the Aqua Mafia clown. "Your death won't change anything. They'll get what they want, with or without you."

"Well then, I guess they'll have to find another way." Arthur nodded.

His decision was made. He didn't turn away as the gun leveled at him one last time. The hammer clicked as it pulled back. Silently, he prayed for his tellers to make it out of this unharmed. Once his petition was complete, peace enveloped him.

When push came to shove, he'd held fast to his morals. He would miss his mother, but he knew she'd be proud of him. That was enough.

2

Sirens blaring, Sheriff Rebecca West slid her SUV sideways into the parking lot of the Sandpiper Bank right behind Senior Deputy Hoyt Frost. They both spilled out of their vehicles at nearly the same time. Guns out and at low ready, they trotted toward the front door and posted up to either side.

Deputy Jake Coffey's cruiser screeched to a halt behind Rebecca's, stopping perpendicular to hers. Though she kept her focus ahead of her, she was aware that he and Deputy Viviane Darby awaited instructions. "Coffey, Darby, block off the road with your vehicles. We don't need anyone else joining us and getting caught in the cross fire."

The two deputies backed out of the front lot and parked sideways in the street before bailing out to join her. Rebecca took that time to tap her pen camera and make sure it was recording. If she missed something in the heat of the moment, the video would catch it.

"See anything?" She glanced over at her senior deputy. "Use your pen."

It was ridiculous that they had to resort to using campy

spy gear she bought at the electronics store. By purchasing them discreetly, Rebecca kept their existence hidden from the corrupt politicians who had access to her spending budget. Sadly, the pens merely approximated the body cameras her team deserved.

Hoyt shook his head and gestured to his left before tapping his own pen.

Stationed to the left of the entrance, she positioned her deputies. "Coffey, Darby, windows."

"On it, Sheriff." Viviane must have seen what Hoyt had done, or maybe she was merely better at remembering, because she also turned her camera on, as did Jake.

Jake ran to her left and Viviane to her right, cutting through the shrubbery between the sidewalk and building. Viviane crouched beneath a reinforced window.

Through the tinted glass doors, Rebecca could see the lobby. Empty of people, it looked like a hurricane had recently passed through. The floor was covered in glossy pamphlets and scattered papers. One section was littered with pink and yellow bits that she thought might be sweetener packets, but that could be her mind responding to the overwhelming scent of coffee in the air. It was too damn early in the morning to be doing something like this.

"What the hell happened in there?" Hoyt's mumbled question echoed Rebecca's thoughts. "I don't see anyone."

Rebecca didn't either. She pressed her radio. "Darby, your window looks in at the end of the row of teller stations."

The bushes rustled in protest as Viviane pushed her way through them, peering inside. "I can see behind the counter. No one's back there, but all the teller drawers are open and appear empty."

That wasn't good.

"Darby, Coffey, work your way around to the back and radio what you see." Rebecca reached up and tried the door.

It was locked and rattled softly from the effort. "They should be open."

"Uh, Boss, is that a handle from a coffee pot? But the pot's next to the wall here." Hoyt nodded to his right.

"Someone broke a coffee pot?" Rebecca moved away from the brick wall she'd tucked herself against to get a better view of the rest of the mayhem. There were no signs of life inside.

Around ten minutes had elapsed since the silent alarm had triggered.

"There goes my hope of this being a false alarm." Hoyt shot her a worried look.

Most alarms were false, but there was a lot wrong with this scene. This felt real. The lack of employees was troublesome. Until she could get eyes on every employee—hell, even *one* employee at this point—she couldn't be certain there were no hostages.

"No, I don't think this is a false alarm either." Rebecca cued her radio. "Coffey, what do you see?"

"Nothing yet." There was a scratch of branches on fabric. "There's nothing down this way, no windows or anything else."

Rebecca knew this was the bank that handled the Yacht Club members' accounts, along with who knew what else. A secure vault on the other side of the lobby housed the cash safe and safety deposit boxes, which could easily hold millions. Perhaps that was where the bank employees were hiding. The inner door to that vault was closed, so she couldn't know until they entered the building.

She craned her neck to search for any signs of movement. "There are cars in the lot, so we know someone should be here. They're supposed to open at nine today, and that was half an hour ago. Where is everyone?"

"There aren't many places they could be. I've only ever

been in the lobby." Viviane's voice whispered through the radio.

"I don't want to pound on the glass. We need to assume there's a robber in there." They had to be prepared for anything. Switching her gun to one hand, Rebecca reached for her radio. "Dispatch, contact the security company for that silent alarm. Ask them if they can tell us what happened in there."

"Already did, Boss. I'm on the phone with them now." Elliot sounded nervous, and Rebecca couldn't blame him. Bank robberies were big-time felony business, technically under FBI jurisdiction. They rarely ended well. "Until they get the camera feed pulled, all they can say for sure is that the alarm did go off. The reset wasn't triggered, and no one from the bank has called in to say it was a false alarm."

"Stay on it and keep us updated." Rebecca braced her gun with both hands again.

Hoyt shook his head. "These doors are reinforced to withstand a hurricane, Boss. So are the windows. There's no way we're opening them without the Jaws of Life or a cutting torch."

She was afraid of that. "We need to find a way in. The longer this goes on without hearing from anyone inside, the more certain I am that—"

"Back door is ajar," Viviane whispered.

Rebecca bolted for the side Viviane had taken, motioning for Coffey to guard the locked door as she and Hoyt ran for the back.

"Elliot, let Coastal Ridge PD know we've got a bank robbery in progress. Suspect is not in sight. Close down the bridge to all westbound traffic."

3

Rebecca's radio chirped, and she prayed it was good news.

"Sheriff, Locke and Abner are en route." Elliot's voice was somewhat steadier. "Should I send them to you or the bridge?"

They weren't SWAT, but she'd take the extra support.

"Send Locke to us, Abner to the roadblock." Rebecca responded as she ran. "And send medical."

The rear of the bank butted up against a lightly wooded area. A short concrete ramp led up to the back door. There was a crack in the concrete, with one side jutting up barely enough to catch the bottom of the metal door.

Viviane's focus appeared to be locked on the entry, but she stepped aside as Rebecca and Hoyt approached. She was still technically in her training period, with Hoyt as her training officer. Rebecca was glad to see her following procedure.

The door was only open a crack, barely enough to get a finger into. Rebecca nodded to Hoyt, the tallest of them.

With a return nod, he stepped forward. His long fingers

gripped the edge of the door and he turned to her, waiting for her directions.

"Dispatch, we're about to make entry." Rebecca made eye contact with the other two, who both raised their weapons into position. Hoyt reached out but waited for Rebecca to give the go ahead.

"State police are five minutes out."

It was tempting to wait, but in situations like this, minutes meant lives.

"Darby, you remember how to clear a building?"

Viviane nodded, confidence flaring in her dark eyes. "I sure do."

"Then you go first and open any closed door so we can clear it."

When they were in position, Rebecca nodded, and Hoyt yanked the door open. The hallway was empty and silent.

Viviane crouched slightly and raised her weapon to shoulder height before walking in. Rebecca followed behind her, and Hoyt brought up the rear, watching their six.

Moving deliberately, Viviane walked heel to toe down the well-lit hall. They passed a large metal box that looked to be an electrical panel and reached a closed, narrow door. She stepped past it, stopping on the hinge side, and reached for the knob.

Rebecca gave her a nod and Viviane pulled the door open. It was a small supply closet. The shelves were mounted directly on the walls, affording no places to hide among the paper towels, coffee cups, and toilet paper. She shook her head.

Viviane moved on. "Open door on the left."

They could all see it coming, but Viviane followed standard operating procedure by calling it out. Rebecca stepped up as Viviane swung the door wide to gain the fullest possible view of the left side of the room.

"Victim down." Viviane's voice squeaked, and she cleared her throat.

Rebecca covered the right side of the room and stepped in. Viviane swung to face the lobby, covering them as they checked the bloody man on the floor.

His shirt was a sopping mess, and Rebecca checked his neck for a pulse. She had to hold her breath to even feel it. "He's alive. Frost, my hand's not big enough, but he's about to bleed to death."

"Dammit. That's Arthur Carson." Hoyt stepped in and dropped to a kneel. He secured his gun and snapped a pair of gloves into place before flipping Arthur's suit jacket back, searching for the source of the blood. A set of keys fell out, hitting the floor with a rattle.

The sound jangled Rebecca's nerves, reminding her of the employees still unaccounted for. She made note of the keys but left them where they landed.

"Stay here and do your best. We'll clear the building. Elliot should have medical en route by now."

Hoyt grunted and jerked Arthur Carson's shirt open.

Gritting her teeth at having to leave this wounded man lying on the floor, Rebecca stepped out of the way.

The hallway only ran another few feet before it opened into the lobby. She made eye contact with Locke and Jake, standing outside the front windows, and jerked her chin to indicate the service counter. They both shook their heads. They hadn't seen anything.

Moving forward, she and Viviane had to slide their feet on the floor, knocking debris and papers aside, to avoid slipping and falling. They came to the first of two doors, this one boasting a heavy outer vault door, open for the day's business. Viviane opened the inner door, revealing the safety deposit box room. Behind a locked gate, lockboxes lined two walls. There was no place for anyone to hide.

Rebecca shook her head and stepped back. Viviane had her gun pointed at the last door, covering Rebecca's back, knowing Jake was keeping watch through the front doors. At her boss's nod, she stepped forward and pushed the door open. It barely moved as it struck something.

The room erupted in screams.

Viviane's shoulders went rigid.

Through the barely ajar door, Rebecca spotted a woman wearing a pale-pink tailored blouse lying with her cheek on the bathroom floor.

The woman's face relaxed when she spied the uniform. She pushed herself up and onto her knees. "My name is Jennifer Wazalski. Jen, please. I'm the head teller." Jen scooted forward to make room for them to open the door.

Rebecca put her gun in her holster and pushed the door until it was flat against the wall. She reached forward, helping Jen to her feet.

Taking her lead, Viviane holstered her weapon before helping the other women. She began cutting the tape that bound their wrists.

"Can you tell me what happened?" Rebecca glanced around the small enclosure.

Jen rubbed her reddened wrists. "Just as we were about to open, a man in a clown costume pushed his way in. He had a gun."

"He was insane," one of the other tellers spat before breaking out into fresh sobs.

Jen wrapped her arm around the crying woman. "Despite the fact that we were doing everything he asked, he trashed the lobby while we gathered all the money from the tills. At one point, it looked like he was reading instructions from a cheat sheet. Like he didn't know what he was doing or something."

"He took Art," the other teller wailed.

Jen scrunched up her face. "Art's the bank manager. I heard a gunshot not long ago. You've got to help him!"

"One of my deputies is tending to him now. Jen, how many people are in the bank? Were there any customers? How many robbers were there in total?" Rebecca mentally admonished herself for not giving the teller time to answer her question before firing another. She needed to make sure the robber hadn't taken hostages.

"There's the three of us tellers and Art. There was no one else in the building. Art had barely unlocked the door. That guy must've been waiting outside."

Rebecca waited while Jen checked over her shoulder at her other coworker, who was upright and battling tears. She observed the women, attempting to visually assess if anyone might be in shock. They were clearly upset, one close to hyperventilation, but otherwise seemed okay. "Is anyone hurt?"

"No. He didn't hurt any of us." Jen seemed the most composed of the women, causing Rebecca to wonder if she'd ever been victim in a bank robbery before, perhaps before joining Sandpiper.

"What did he look like?"

Jen shook her head, as if she couldn't believe what she was about to say. "He, um. He was a clown. A tall clown."

"Okay." Rebecca nodded, absorbing the information but not quite sure how to respond. She'd worry about tall clowns later, she decided. "Stay here. We're going to get the keys to open the front door, and then, after Deputy Darby finishes helping you get unbound, she'll escort you all out. One of my men will take your statements."

Viviane offered her megawatt smile, and Rebecca knew she was trying to put the women at ease.

Moments later, the foursome stepped away from the bathroom, each of them attempting to avoid the clutter scattered across the lobby. Rebecca directed them out the back. "We don't want to tamper with too much up here and we've already used the rear. Jen, who keeps the keys?"

"Art."

"Okay. I think I saw them in his office. I'll see if I can grab them before the medics haul him off." Rebecca pressed the radio. "Coffey, we've got three women coming out the back. Dispatch, tell that ambulance to step it up. We've got a gunshot wound."

4

After ushering the hostages out the rear door, Viviane had returned to the room where Rebecca was helping Hoyt with Arthur Carson. As unobtrusively as possible, Viviane retrieved his keys.

As soon as the crime scene was secured, she went to the vehicle for her camera. Documenting every detail before it got trampled and contaminated further was a crucial step toward solving the crime. Back in the building, she looked toward the hallway. Hoyt and Rebecca were still in the office, assisting the EMTs who were working hard to keep Arthur Carson alive.

Though she'd barely glanced at the bank manager, Viviane saw the hole in his torso and the black speckles of unburned gunpowder from a close gunshot to the chest.

Inhaling deeply, she counted to four before releasing her breath to a count of six in a controlled, even stream. Her hands weren't shaking, but fine tremors ran up and down her back and shoulders. Trying to hide her jitters, she tucked her thumbs into her belt loops and willed her body to stillness.

Though Viviane had only been on the job a short time, the nightmares had started the day she was sworn in as an officer of the law. Instead of normal nightmares with blood, guts, or rotting bodies, she dreamed of failure, of letting people down. The shrieks of the tellers when she opened the bathroom door would haunt her dreams tonight, she was sure.

As she contemplated the possibility of another night of interrupted sleep, she yawned hugely. Her exhaustion had her in a stranglehold.

"Shake it off, Darby."

Viviane clapped a hand over her open mouth and turned to face Jake, who'd walked up behind her. He was shaking his arms and even kicking a foot out as he shifted his weight back and forth—a one-man Hokey Pokey dance. Literally following his own advice.

"All that tension from making a complicated entry will eat at your body unless you shake it off as soon as possible. You might not notice how tight you're holding your body right away, but trust me, you'll start feeling it soon enough."

She laughed and copied his movements. "You think this is rough? Try sitting at a desk and listening in as this happens and not being able to do anything about it."

He bobbed his head to the side. "Is that why you became a deputy? So you wouldn't have to sit there and just listen?"

"That's one of the reasons." Viviane shrugged her shoulders around in circles while wiggling her fingers.

Doing the same exercises outside was Trent Locke. The man who'd once been the worst deputy in the station was now competent enough for Viviane to feel she could trust him. With everyone else on a first-name basis, it felt wrong to keep calling him "Locke," so she resolved to make him feel part of the crew. Trent moved out to the parking lot to start taking the statements of the three tellers.

She shook out the tension in her arms. "Honestly, though, I never thought I'd be doing something like *this*. I mean, a bank robbery? In our little town? It's surreal."

From childhood, Viviane had wanted to be a deputy. That was because she saw how it was for Wallace, Hoyt, Greg, and her mom as the dispatcher. A bank robbery was something she never expected. Though she loved her new role, she was constantly struggling with the long, odd hours, feeling like she always needed to be "on." The job was even harder when folks she knew personally, like Arthur Carson, were affected.

As she took in the debris in the bank lobby, she felt overwhelmed. If she was doing first aid, she'd at least feel more certain about her actions.

Elliot's voice sparked through their radios. "The FBI should get there soon." Viviane registered the information and cued her mic. Noting a tinge of worry in Elliot's voice, she wanted to reassure him that he'd handled the situation perfectly. She remembered being new on the job and always worrying if she was doing things correctly. It didn't matter that she'd literally grown up at the feet of the previous dispatcher, her mom.

"Great job, Dispatch."

"They're going to have their hands full dealing with this." Jake waved his hand around, indicating the giant mess strewn across the bank lobby. "I don't know where they'll start. It'll take them forever, moving the layers of coffee-covered paper to see what's underneath."

Viviane agreed. She was hopeful that "floors littered with soggy pieces of paper" wouldn't join her growing collection of job-related nightmares. Screaming tellers, on the other hand, were sure to make the list.

"I'm so glad the Feebies will have to deal with the mess. We can just babysit it until they arrive." Jake's chin jerked up. "Speaking of the Blue Coat Squad, there they are now."

Viviane looked out to the road as a black SUV with flashing lights came into view.

"Only one car for now, but I'm sure their forensic people will be here soon enough." Jake walked forward and unlocked the bank door as the FBI pulled into the parking lot.

Viviane had made sure to take pictures of everything before the gurney and EMTs traipsed through the lobby. And the footage from their pen cameras would document the scene through the windows before anyone had disturbed it. Viviane walked out the door to join Jake on the sidewalk.

Looking over at the new arrivals, Viviane stifled a groan. "Oh, damn. It's him."

"Who?" Jake spun around.

She was surprised he'd been able to hear her quiet grumbling. She gestured nonchalantly with her head to an agent getting out of the SUV. They'd at least parked far enough away to not interfere with anything.

"Agent *Too Cocky for His Own Good* Stalwart. He came down back in June when we had those kidnappers and showed his lack of class by trying to take over our case. Reb…the sheriff…had to put him in his place, as he was acting like the Lord himself had sent him."

"This should be fun to watch, then. Boss is in no mood to deal with anyone's crap right now. I think she was friends with the manager." Jake squinted as a second man exited the SUV. This one was tall, and his heavily grayed hair was a striking contrast to his dark skin. "Who's the other guy?"

"No clue." Viviane strolled over to where Trent was leaning against his cruiser, still taking statements from the tellers. She leaned in and dropped her voice so only he could hear her. "Deputy Locke, the FBI is here."

Trent lifted his head and craned to peer around the

parking lot. "Okay. Why are you telling me?" He kept his voice as low as hers.

"Because you're the most senior deputy available right now. You need to be the one to walk them through and sign over the scene until the boss and Senior Deputy Frost can talk to them. And that short one is a real pain in the butt."

Trent straightened, and for a moment she thought she saw a flash of worry in his eyes. "Right. I can do that, but I think you should get Sheriff West. I've never dealt with the FBI before."

Taking a deep breath, he squared his shoulders and went to meet the agents.

Viviane watched his approach. *You got this, Trent.*

5

The two-hour parking spot in the rear of a small grocery store lot near the center of the island was the perfect place to ditch the car. I glanced at the phone again, double-checking that this was the correct location.

Getting step-by-step directions was helpful but also a complete pain in the ass. I didn't like being anyone's lackey—but the money for this job was worth a little humility.

There were only a handful of cars in the parking lot on a Monday at midmorning. Luckily, no one was around to see my strange attire or complain about my parking.

I'd already scrubbed off the makeup I'd worn under the mask. Now that I wore a hairnet, nitrile gloves, and a long chef's coat over baggy pants, I could pass for a deli, bakery, or restaurant worker.

The blood-splattered clown costume, including the booties, cotton gloves, and mask, was in a plastic garbage bag on the passenger floor mat. I picked it up as I climbed out. There were also two giant bottles of hydrogen peroxide, a tub of baby wipes, and a lint roller. On the drive over, I'd stuffed the three bank bags into my generic Rockport backpack.

I opened the peroxide bottles and dumped them into the garbage bag with the clown gear. The peroxide would destroy, or at least damage, any DNA left on the material. Next, I ran a lint roller over every surface of the car's interior, including the carpeted floor mats.

For the entire time I'd had the car, I'd never gotten in without wearing a hairnet, gloves, and discardable clothing. No sense taking chances. I dropped layer after fuzzy layer of lint roller paper into the garbage bag to get sanitized as well.

Next, I wiped down every surface of the interior, making it even cleaner than it had been when I'd picked it up from the rental agency. Those wipes, along with the emptied peroxide bottles and everything else I'd used to clean the car, were all stuffed into the garbage bag. It wasn't until I was walking away, downwind of the car and heading out of the parking lot, that I finally took off the hairnet.

Per the instructions I'd carefully followed, I found waiting for me one of those new Dodge Rams with the chrome bumper guards that flared out along the sides. Walking around it, I casually jammed the bag of evidence into the side flange.

Pulling my burner phone, I sent the text I'd been avoiding this whole time.

Mission complete. Target neutralized. Primary objective remains. Virus not uploaded. Plan B?

My employer would be unhappy. Ensuring the financial transfers had been the primary purpose of the mission.

I'd been instructed to upload a ghost virus to the bank manager's computer if he refused to do the transfers. The virus would make my employer's accounts appear to vanish from the system. My handlers only told me what I needed to know, but I was young and savvy enough to understand how these things worked. They'd need a decryption key to retrieve the "missing" files. Likely once the heat died down from the robbery.

The robbery itself was the first half of my payment. I'd been promised double my take if I successfully unleashed the computer virus on the system.

Unfortunately, I'd run out of time. When I'd searched for the master power switch to Carson's computer, I'd seen the silent alarm had been triggered. There was no way I was sticking around long enough to upload their virus.

I shifted the backpack on my shoulders, feeling the weight of the stolen cash. It was probably enough for my purposes, if I was honest with myself. But doubling would be so much sweeter. Finishing the job meant more money…and a smaller probability of someone killing me in my sleep in a couple weeks.

I'd pressed the start button on the Ram already, prepared to ditch the contents of my evidence bag along the coast.

A moment or two later, a response—new instructions—lit up my phone screen.

Stay on the island.

That was the last thing I wanted to do. This place would be hopping with Feds soon. I already heard sirens in the distance.

Still, these guys were the experts. They must've had some kind of misdirection planned.

Per the new directions dinging on my phone, I turned the Ram to the main street of Shadow Island.

For the next half hour, I drove to random parts of the island—a pier here, an empty beach there, an old boathouse—finding the most isolated places to dump the evidence, bit by bit, into the ocean. Except for the gun. Guns were handy.

After discarding the clown wig in the marshes, I blew out a relieved breath. Even if it washed up on the beaches, between the saltwater and the peroxide, it'd be a miracle if the cops found any DNA.

I made it to a small roadway near the docks. Parking the truck, I texted my contact, letting him know where his people could pick it up. After stashing the thumb drive in my Rockport, I abandoned the Ram.

Apparently, the Yacht Club had several drivers to just pick up and abandon vehicles whenever they wanted.

As casually as I could, I glanced around, as if checking traffic. When I didn't see anyone paying the slightest bit of attention to a random worker heading for the sidewalk, I jerked at the waistband of my tearaway pants.

Metal snaps along both sides gave way. It took one more tug to break them loose from my ankles. The back half of the pants fell onto the asphalt of the parking lot, and the front half dropped on the curb as I walked away. Already, I was halfway to my destination and most of the secondary costume was gone.

As I walked past a small restaurant, I removed my coat and dropped it in the garbage can without slowing.

I sat down on a bench and leaned forward to rest my forearms on my knees. For anyone watching, I looked like any other dude going to or from work while I stared at my phone and waited for a response.

Now that it was all said and done, I had nothing else to focus on except the events of that morning.

My hands started shaking as the adrenaline surge began to recede. Stripping the gloves, I tossed them behind the bench I was sitting on.

In spite of being safe, my heart wouldn't stop attempting to thump out of my chest.

At the last second in the bank manager's office, knowing what I had to do, I'd closed my eyes, pulled the trigger, and never looked at his body again. I didn't need the mental image of the mess my gun had made of the man. Attempting to go about my task in his office, I averted my eyes from the unmoving body.

Still, I'd felt the jerk of the recoil when I'd pulled the trigger. I'd probably feel that sharp motion every day until I died.

Dammit! It wasn't supposed to go that way. I'd known it was a possibility when I'd taken the job. Yet it had never once occurred to me that Carson would refuse the deal.

Albert Gilroy had given me the same choice, and it'd been a no-brainer. But there hadn't been a second of hesitation from the bank manager as he stared directly into my soul and rejected the offer.

His words echoed in my head. *"Life is worth more than money. Which is why I will never do what they want. Kill me if you have to. I will never help you or them."*

If Carson had done what he was told, I wouldn't have had to kill him. The Yacht Club would prefer to have a man on the inside of the bank instead of a dead man they couldn't use.

I hoped they wouldn't be too pissed that their accounts were still exposed. I'd fix it—but they needed to help me help them.

As if to answer my question, the next text was an address, along with two words that brought me comfort.

Safe house.

I breathed a sigh of relief. They weren't mad. Staying on the island was just part of the plan. I could lay low for a bit, then tackle uploading the virus a different way.

Maybe, when everything was said and done, I'd get my second payment and perhaps even get a ride out in one of those fancy boats.

Carson was wrong. Life was worth nothing without money.

6

Rebecca and Hoyt had done their best to stay out of the way in the cramped room once the EMTs arrived. After the medics had taken over the job of resuscitation, Rebecca and her senior deputy squeezed past them and out of the bank manager's office.

Her arms were shaking from the strain of what she'd gone through, and if she hadn't been leaning against the wall in the hallway, she was certain her knees would have given out.

Viviane approached Rebecca but had to jump out of the way as Arthur Carson was finally rolled out of the bank in a hurry.

"Hey, Boss, the Feds are here." She hooked a thumb over her shoulder toward the front door.

"I think she means me." The speaker's voice was familiar, coming from a tall man with gray hair and dark skin walking up behind Viviane. Rebecca recognized him and the twinkle of mischief in his brown eyes right away.

Viviane startled and spun around. "Oh, I was just getting the sheriff for you."

"Sorry to have startled you. And Rebecca, it's good to see that you're taking it easy and not working too hard. Your Deputy Locke told me where I could find you."

Rebecca's sour mood instantly lightened. "Benson! How the hell are you?" She plucked at her blood-smeared uniform. "Yeah, I'm being lazy, standing around, relaxing, dabbling in some therapeutic finger painting. You know how it goes." She rubbed her sweaty palms on her pant legs before extending her hand to shake.

"That was pretty dark, even for you." Benson shook her proffered hand. "I figured you had to be bored down here if you found the time to send a glitter bomb to my house. Not sure if you heard, but I opened it in my work car. Pink sparkles still erupt every time I pull the seat belt down."

"You sent me a rookie agent and let him think he could take over my kidnapping case. He walked into my crime scene and wouldn't show his badge or ID. He struggled to comprehend I was the sheriff at first. You're lucky I didn't toss him in a cell and make you come fetch him. I felt a glitter bomb exemplified my appreciation for that."

Rebecca turned to Hoyt, who was leaning against the wall, still catching his breath after giving CPR for the last eight minutes. No doubt he was a bit lightheaded as well.

"Senior Deputy Frost, let me introduce you to Special Agent in Charge Prankster Benson."

"Sir." Hoyt gave him a brief nod as he shot a confused glance at Rebecca.

She loved pranking her coworkers, but Hoyt was far more gullible than Benson. "He was one of my instructors, back when I was a rookie Fed and he was a lowly special agent. He's also the one who thought it was a good idea to send Agent Stalwart to us so I could beat him into shape before sending him back to the Bureau."

Benson rolled his eyes at Rebecca and gave a short wave

to Hoyt. "It's Special Agent in Charge *Percy* Benson. I think the prankster moniker is better suited for your sheriff here."

"What's in a name, Perce?" Rebecca saw Benson's eyes narrow, and she knew he was planning retribution. They'd been trading pranks for her entire career, and it was his turn now. "How'd you make it down so fast? And why you? Surely there are more important things for a SAC to do."

"We happened to be close by on a training exercise. The rest of them are on their way and will be here shortly. I've got six special agents coming to join me." Benson shrugged, as if it were no big deal. And for a SAC used to dealing with more than a hundred agents, it was a small number. "Oh, and Agent Stalwart is here too."

Hoyt snorted and shook his head. "That's about as useful as a fart in the bathtub."

"Are you still hoping I'll knock some sense into him?" Rebecca raised an eyebrow at her old friend. "I kind of have my hands full right now. Unless you plan to take this case over, since bank robberies are your jurisdiction?"

"I just got here. I'm not willing to make that decision yet. We can work together and figure out what happened here. Did your victim pull through?"

"Time will tell. Arthur Carson, fifty-one years old, bank manager. Deputy Frost and I performed CPR until we handed him over to the EMTs. Those were the folks who ran past you with the gurney. Carson lost a lot of blood and appears to have suffered a beating before he was shot."

Rebecca glanced over her shoulder into the bank manager's office, taking in the mess left by the paramedics. Carson had been lying on top of scattered papers and knickknacks from his desk and shelves, all covered in his blood now. "We've done what we could to preserve the scene, but there's been a lot of action around here."

"I can see that. The lobby looks about the same." Benson

surveyed the destruction that had been spread to every corner of the bank.

Rebecca shook her head. "It was like that when we got here. Jennifer Wazalski, one of three tellers who were confined to the bathroom while this happened, said the robber went berserk and was trashing the place, even though they were complying with his orders."

"She's the one with brown hair and a pink top." Hoyt nodded at the SAC before picking his way past them, heading toward the front.

Rebecca followed, but at a much slower pace. "Let me give you a quick rundown of what happened before you got here. We got the call just after nine twenty. Deputy Frost and I arrived here at approximately nine thirty. We saw the mess in the lobby, but the doors were locked. Deputy Darby went around the back and found a door, which was ajar."

Benson navigated around a larger pile of deposit slips on the floor as he listened.

"We made entry and found Carson. Then we cleared the rest of the building and found three women, Wazalski and the other two tellers. They'd been bound and forced to lie on their bellies in the bathroom. She stated that the robber left them in there before taking Carson away. She also thinks she heard the gunshot that struck him in the chest, which preliminary evidence indicates was at close range."

"He brought the man to his office to kill him?"

They were along the edge of the lobby, taking it all in. Everything was a mess, and Agent Stalwart, the data analyst who'd made such a bad impression on them a few months prior, was standing in the middle of it like a stranded leaf in a churning river.

"Beat him and kill him. Not sure why yet. Before I began CPR, I noticed one of the ribs flexed strangely on his side. I'm certain the chest compressions we administered did even more damage to his ribs. And while I was on the ground, I saw that there's a silent alarm in his office. It was recessed."

Rebecca kept watch of where she placed each foot but made sure not to step on anything else. "I'm guessing Carson managed to trigger it during the altercation. Maybe that's why he was shot."

"Smart thinking on his part. From the looks of things, the reason he's alive is because you and your crew got here in time."

Rebecca stared at his familiar square face, listening to that calm, strong voice that had been her lifeline when she'd struggled with her job after the death of her parents. Everyone else had wanted her to hurry up, get over it, and move on. Only Benson had been willing to listen to her. He'd even helped her piece together some of the information that ultimately led to her finding those responsible.

"It's good to see you again, Benson."

"It's good to see you too, West."

She debated if she should share what she'd been dealing with since leaving the Bureau. Tell him everything she had on her plate, how pervasive and far-reaching all the crimes linked to this small town were. Maybe she should get his advice, possibly even his expertise and help.

"Hey, Sheriff, Deputy Frost needs you out here." Locke motioned to her from the front door as more black SUVs pulled into the lot.

The rest of the FBI had arrived.

7

"We should probably go out the back and walk around the building instead of tracking through this mess again." Rebecca gestured to the lobby and the utter chaos wrought there. Their path to the front doors of the bank was an obstacle course.

Agent Stalwart, appearing a bit shell-shocked, stared at Benson and Rebecca. He was still wearing his navy blue jacket with *FBI* written on the back, and his hair was still plastered down and smoothed flat, though it was even shorter than the last time she'd seen him.

Benson glanced down at Rebecca's bloody attire and nodded. "The scene is already compromised enough. No sense making it worse. Agent Stalwart, walk out the same way you came in and meet us over by the cars."

"Yes, sir." Stalwart turned and started carefully picking his way to the doors.

Heading for the back, Rebecca untucked her uniform top and pulled it away from her skin. There wasn't a lot of blood on her, but enough that she wanted to get into clean clothes as soon as possible.

"If the tellers were locked up, did they push the silent alarm before then?" Benson kept his stride shorter to match hers, something she appreciated. Too many men didn't bother to show that kind of respect.

He was asking her the same question as before but wording it differently. She didn't mind, though. Benson wasn't trying to trip her up or catch her in a lie. Instead, it was a way to make sure her memory of the events was consistent after her recent adrenaline rush. "As far as we can tell, it was Carson's desk alarm that was triggered. But we'll have to check with the security company to say for certain."

"You think that's the reason the robber beat Carson?" He squinted as they stepped into the bright morning sunshine.

Rebecca had already thought this through. "It's possible. We might never know, if Carson doesn't pull through. My suspicion is that Carson was being beaten. Why, I couldn't tell you. He found an opportunity while down on the ground and somehow pressed the alarm."

Benson nodded. "You think it's possible the robber saw that, shot him, and then fled?"

"Yeah." She shielded her eyes from the sun as she peered around the street. "Because many of the scattered papers landed on top of some of the blood splatters, I think the beating happened, at least in part, before some of the destruction. Also, I'm pretty certain there was something wet on the alarm button. It glistened. If testing comes back and shows blood, more specifically Carson's blood, then we'll know he sustained some injuries before triggering the alarm."

Benson wrote something down in his notebook. "Good catch."

Rebecca rolled her head to stretch out her neck muscles. "Once your crew tests the blood in the office, we'll know if it matches Carson or if it belongs to the robber. But I doubt we'd get that lucky. I didn't see any abrasions on the bank manager's knuckles that would indicate he got in any blows of his own."

Benson raised his hand, catching his team's attention as they rounded the corner of the building. "Any theories on why our unsub would beat Carson?"

"No idea." Rebecca gave a bit of a nod to the six agents who were waiting for their SAC before doing anything else. She raised her voice so they could all hear. "The teller said they gave him the money from the tills, then he herded them into the bathroom. Clearly, he wanted something in addition to the cash."

"Any idea of what it could be?"

"Not yet." Rebecca continued to move toward the assembled group. "With the giant mess he made everywhere, it's hard to tell if something's missing or moved. And I didn't spend long in the lobby anyway. As soon as we were clear, I went back to administer first aid."

"Understandable. You did good, West."

Ignoring the compliment, Rebecca spotted her people off to the side, gathered around the cruisers and the three tellers. "You can ask Deputies Darby, Coffey, and Locke. They took over with the witnesses while I was in back with Senior Deputy Frost."

Benson nodded, then pointed at three of his people. "Go reinterview the witnesses. And the rest of you can go process the scene. I want every paper, every shard, every business card, including all the coffee-drenched stuff, catalogued and plotted. There's already been some foot traffic through there, so we'll need to take samples from the EMTs and the deputies as well. I want to know if the robber tried to get into the vault, the ATM, the safety deposit boxes, the bank manager's desk, or any of the computers."

"I can get you pictures of the lobby before it was compromised," Rebecca offered.

When Benson opened his mouth to ask a question, she shook her head at him, not willing to publicly discuss the pen cameras they used in place of body cameras. The secret cameras had already helped gather information that could be used later, and she didn't want word of them getting out.

Rebecca pointed to the ATM. "That machine has a camera in it, as well, but it only records while in use. I doubt it'll be useful in this case."

Benson stared at the six agents still standing in front of him.

They stared back.

Rebecca raised an eyebrow. "Are you waiting for the scene to dry up and the witnesses to die of old age? You've been given your tasks, now move!"

They startled and finally took off, only one glancing back to check with Benson to see if it was okay that they were following her orders. Benson shooed him along.

"Trainees. I had to be out with the newest batch before coming down here."

Rebecca languidly stretched her arms and rocked back on her heels. "Yeah. That's too bad. It's also too bad that this scene's going to be such a complete pain in the ass to run forensics on." Her tone was saccharin sweet. "Just like it's so sad that this is your crime scene now and not mine. Bank robbery has FBI jurisdiction written all over it."

"Measured response." That was Benson's only reply, but she knew exactly what he meant.

In March 2001, the FBI implemented a measured response initiative. It was designed to lessen the FBI's workload and turn over some of the investigation to local police for bank robberies that were less violent.

The Feds were still required to show up for bank

robberies, and they always did. But the robber's use of a gun meant the FBI would have to do more than just put in an appearance, measured response notwithstanding. Benson was razzing her—his favorite pastime.

"Oh, come on." Rebecca's tone was mock-offended. "My entire staff is the same size as your initial team." She pointed at the four deputies standing by watching them hash things out. "It's me, those four, and a man I pulled out of retirement to help train my rookies. You passed him on the bridge into town. If you drop this in my lap, I won't be able to cover anything else that happens on this island for the next three days."

Benson shrugged. "Measured response." He walked away as she stared after him. "I'm not saying I'll hand it over immediately. But who can say what the future holds? Don't forget, I trained you. I'm sure you can handle it if you put your mind to it."

Sure, the robbery had fallen within Rebecca's jurisdiction. Anyone determined to add this to the "crime wave" that was being investigated by Special Agent Rhonda Lettinger could do that whether Benson took over the case or not. And she didn't want to give the appearance of shirking her duties. Civilians wouldn't know or care whether this was technically her case. Reluctantly, she followed him.

"Tell you what." Benson turned around, and she eyed her mentor. "Since I did saddle you with Stalwart, and you did manage to convince him that his skills worked best in the office like I wanted, I'll be nice this time. Leave me one of your newbies. They can get a good look at how these things are done, and I'll have a local to help out. Sound like a deal?"

"Since I'm sure your decision has nothing to do with the fact that the robber brandished a firearm," she paused to let him know she understood the intricacies of measured response, "I'm happy to take that deal."

"But I still reserve the right to hand this over once we've done the heavy lifting."

"Of course. And Darby is my newest, still working with her training officer. But she's smart as a whip and can learn anything you want to teach her. She's all yours for the day. I have admin duties at the station, a budget with some surplus, and an antiquated building aching to be brought out of the dark ages."

If she was lucky, Benson would handle this case all the way to the end.

Not that she was ever lucky.

8

Rebecca had finished changing into clean clothes in the locker room and was getting coffee out in the bullpen as Greg Abner walked in.

Greg glared disapprovingly at Rebecca. "So the Feebies are taking over the whole case?" He scrubbed at his overnight growth of a scruffy mustache as he dropped into his seat in the back of the bullpen.

Rebecca kept drinking her coffee, relishing the caffeine as it chased away the lethargy that'd been settling in. Sleep had become elusive for the last couple of days, with the morning not making things any easier. "They have every right to do so."

"But we still have to write up reports for them to read. What the heck is that about?" Locke groused as he glared at his computer monitor.

Jake responded before Rebecca could. "We were the responding officers. They need to know what we saw and did on the scene so they can figure out what they're working with."

"That's right. Also, you guys do realize they're doing the

heavy lifting while we sit on our butts and write up the reports we'd have to do anyway. Right?"

Locke and Greg turned to her with puzzled expressions.

"Locke, you saw that scene. They're the ones picking through with a fine-tooth comb, breaking their backs at it instead of us. I pushed for that because I knew the forensics was going to be an all-day, all-night event."

Greg turned to Locke and got a nod of agreement. "How the hell? The bank isn't that big. Or did they only bring a couple guys down?"

"The robber trashed the entire place. And beat the crap out of Arthur Carson, the bank manager, before shooting him in the chest." Hoyt came out from the hallway that led to the interrogation and locker rooms. He, too, had changed into a clean uniform.

"Yep. And with the FBI taking the lead, they get cleanup duty. The use of a firearm should keep this in the FBI's lap, but they could hand us mop-up duty. Or we might find ourselves working with them on this one." Rebecca handed Hoyt a mug of coffee as he nodded his thanks.

But Greg kept pressing the issue. "If we work together, who's going to take lead on that?"

"That would be me. For the moment, Benson is in charge, and we'll share evidence with them." Rebecca finished topping off her cup. She still needed to write her own reports. "Greg, Locke, if you want, you can go home and write your report this evening on your normal shift."

Locke jerked around and went back to typing. "Nah, that's fine. I'll finish this first. But then I might go back to the scene. Vi's still there getting training on federal cases, right? I was thinking of swinging by. Maybe there's something I can help with."

This was the first time Locke had ever volunteered for anything, and Rebecca wasn't about to tell him no. He'd recently finished his remedial training and was still being overseen by Greg for most of his night shifts. So far, Greg had found very few things he'd needed to correct the man on. Recently, Greg hadn't even been griping about anything except the hours cutting into his fishing time.

Rebecca shot a glance at Hoyt, but he silently shook his head. He didn't know what was going on either.

"That's up to you. It's okay with me if that's what you decide. Consider the overtime pay approved. Frost, once you're done, you can help me go through the CCTV footage from the bank and nearby stores."

The bullpen remained silent as she walked to her own office. She left the door open, as usual, but didn't hear anything other than the clicks and clacks of keyboards. There was a stack of papers waiting for her approval to move forward with the required renovations to the station, but instead she turned on her computer. Her inbox showed a few emails from the bank's security company. The last one showed the subject line, *Read first*.

Thinking that was a damn fine place to start, Rebecca opened the email.

There was a video attached, along with two stills from the recording. The first was a picture of a car in front of the bank. The image quality was good enough that Rebecca identified the car as a Mitsubishi Mirage. In the next picture, a clown carrying a gun was getting out of the driver's seat.

Yeah. As creepy as this case was shaping up to be, she was more than happy to let Benson deal with this circus. A sleep-deprived idea occurred to her, and she was suddenly curious if more and more clowns would get out of the car when she played the video.

They didn't.

She ran the plates to see if she got a hit. There was no

time to wish for it to be registered to Barnum or Bailey before she got a result. The car was a rental.

Bingo. She picked up her phone to let Benson know what she'd discovered. The sooner they got a BOLO out, the sooner they could catch the clown. As early as the day was, this case might even be wrapped up before tomorrow.

9

My designated safe house was large and expensive as hell. This was one of the nicest places I'd ever crashed in.

One day I'd have a house like this. I hefted the Rockport, feeling the weight of the cash already in my possession.

My parents would never understand wanting this kind of a place. They were too focused on pulling themselves up by their bootstraps to know what true prosperity could be.

This was what I wanted. To live easy in a magnificent house. It was an older home that looked like it'd been remodeled and upgraded over the years. The garage added on to the side was big enough to hold at least three cars.

The backyard was spacious with several trees—tall junipers providing some cover. Nothing basic like a chain-link or wooden slat fence for whoever lived here. Albert had directed me to head through those trees when I'd asked how I was supposed to approach a house in this neighborhood.

Whoever lived here had focused more on style and prestige than they had on security and sensibility. Most people would've sprung for locked gates and guard dogs.

I checked the phone again as I approached the shed.

According to Albert, there was supposed to be a spare key hidden in a can on the bottom left shelf. The lock on the shed door wasn't engaged. It was only lined up to give the illusion of being locked.

I twisted the base, lifted the lock off, and swung open the shed door. Despite the rows of tools hanging on the walls, there wasn't a hint of sawdust in the air. Stepping in, I spotted a framing hammer on the workbench next to a pile of heavily dented wood.

Looked like someone got frustrated with their project.

The can stood out like a rowboat at a yacht club. A coffee can without a lid sat next to bins of unopened packets of screws. I retrieved the key, closed the workshop, and left it the same way I'd found it.

I let myself into the house through the back door, which led to a very modern kitchen.

Each floor tile was painted with a different design. It must have cost a small fortune. *Who paints the floor they're going to walk on?* Flicking on the light switch showed the house was fully furnished, which I hadn't expected.

Hesitating before I stepped farther in, I pulled out my phone.

Are you sure no one lives here?

I hit send and waited. Patience was one of my virtues.

But I didn't have to wait long.

Yes.

How do you know?

Because the owner's head is currently in a box at the bottom of the ocean.

What'd he do?

Didn't follow directions.

"Noted," I murmured.

There was more of a story there, but I was not about to press my luck. Instead, my stomach guided me to the fridge.

Most of the veggies had turned into piles of rot. The stench was unbelievable. I closed the door and gave myself a small tour, leaving my bag of money sitting on the kitchen table. Considering the abandoned state of the place, I couldn't imagine anyone walking in and stealing my stolen cash.

Pieces of artwork decorated every wall, and there were several antiques throughout the house. Wealth plastered all over in a display that made me think of peacocks. I'd been warned to stay away from the front windows, but as I walked into the den with its massive leather recliners and gigantic flat screen, I found the curtains were shut tight.

It only took a bit more wandering to find a bathroom, and I finally got to wash up. The day had been long, and I was exhausted. All I wanted now was a drink, food, and then bed. Even though I'd worn a disguise, there was no way I was going to venture out for dinner.

Drying my hands on a towel, I strolled back to the kitchen. The fridge was a waste of time, so I checked the freezer. Everything in it seemed fine. No ice crystals growing out of control or bad smells. There were even ice cubes in the dispenser.

Steak and fries sounded perfect. I tossed one of the steaks into the microwave to thaw and wandered back to the bar in the den. This was the life. A crystal bottle filled with a brown liquid and topped with a stopper stood on a small liquor table. I grabbed one of the short, fancy glasses that matched the bottle and filled it.

Drink in hand, I wandered around the den. Solid wood shelves were lined with sports memorabilia. There were a couple baseball bats laid out. And an entire shelf was dedicated to signed baseballs enshrined in glass cases. Leaning in for a better view, I saw one that had a Ty Cobb autograph.

Sipping my drink, I popped the case open with my free hand and lifted the baseball. I went over to my backpack and added it to my own little collection of valuables.

Clearly, working with the Yacht Club had its advantages. The bank manager had been a fool to reject the offer. Working for them ensured that I had everything I needed and most of what I wanted. All it cost me was a few days of planning and one day of actual work.

I dropped into the leather chair and ran my hands over it. Soft and supple, it still smelled like a tanner's workshop.

I was a made man. Not only did I have the money from the bank I'd robbed that morning and my new Ty Cobb baseball, I had the rest of my previous "earnings" as well. After this job was done, once Albert got me off the island, I could go down to Mexico and tan on the beach.

Maybe I'd even buy a place like this down there.

Tomorrow, my entire life would change.

10

"You know that as the boss, no one's ever going to question you if you show up late, right?" Special Agent in Charge Benson tapped on the doorframe to Rebecca's office to get her attention. "Your dispatcher said you came in early this morning."

"Yeah, well, Humphrey wanted a nap after our morning run. After that, I figured I might as well come in and get some paperwork done."

Benson handed her a cup of coffee. "Is that the name of your new man?"

Rebecca was amused at the guess, and it wasn't far off. She was starting to think that the best part of having Ryker staying with her was Humphrey. "Close enough. He's my boyfriend's dog. Ryker was still sleeping when I left. He's recovering from a traumatic brain injury and staying with me until he gets better."

She took a sip of her coffee and spit it out, spluttering. As her tongue tried to shrivel up, she knew she'd fallen for his prank.

Benson leaned back in his chair, his own cup hiding the

smirk she heard in his voice. "Ah, the old salt in the coffee trick. Gets you every time." He pulled a stack of napkins from his pocket and set them on her desk. "I can't believe you still fall for that."

Rebecca glared at his stoic face. She knew he was laughing at her on the inside, but he kept his expression perfectly neutral. That was the real reason he always managed to pull the same tricks on her. That and the fact that she'd been lulled into complacency by working with decent people who didn't prank each other in such ways. She picked up the napkin and started to wipe her mouth, then froze.

Chili pepper flakes spilled from the folded napkin onto her desk, floating in the little puddles of coffee she'd spit out.

"Well, I guess you can be taught after all." Benson sipped his coffee nonchalantly. "It only took you a few years and a couple hundred cups of coffee with peppered napkins."

Using the napkins to wipe off her desk instead, Rebecca flung them into her trash can. "You know I'm going to get you back for that." She crossed her arms and leaned forward on her desk.

"Maybe, but I also know you're going to be paranoid about your coffee for the rest of the day. Totally worth it. Watching an addict not getting her fix because of her own anxiety." He slurped and smacked his lips. "That's mighty tasty."

"I still can't believe you manage to pass the psych eval every time." Rebecca pushed the salt-laced coffee to the side so she wouldn't accidentally pick it up again, making a mental note to dump it in the bathroom sink when she got a chance. "Did you manage to track down that car I sent you the plate for?"

"It took a while, but we tracked it to an agency in Coastal Ridge, Virginia." Now that the joke was over, amusement danced in Benson's eyes. "They were closed by then and hadn't filed the paperwork with the chain, which was why it took so long to track it down. My team is still working on the physical evidence inside the bank. You think you can get your people to run the rental down?"

"Sure." Rebecca made another mental note. "Have you gone over the footage I uploaded into the file?"

"Not all of it. I skimmed the rest of it knowing you'd take care of all of that and give me the play-by-play over coffee. But I did watch where the clown was outside and charged his way in." He gestured at the door. "Besides, Stalwart'll be here soon. And I'm certain he's already gone through every digital piece of evidence."

"What about the physical evidence? Did you manage to find anything of note in all that?" Rebecca reached out for the cup of coffee, then remembered herself. She didn't want to give Benson the satisfaction, but there was a small smile on his lips nonetheless.

"Not yet."

"I think you might want to reach out to Special Agent Rhonda Lettinger of the Bureau of Criminal Investigation with the state police. She recently served a warrant to that bank. I'm not sure for what case. You can ask her, though." Rebecca wrote down Rhonda's number and slid it over to him. "Carson had implied he might have information I could use, as well, but I never got a case that would allow me a warrant to investigate it. And Carson was a stickler for rules."

He took the note and stared at it. "You said it was already served? Did she get what she wanted?"

Rebecca pointed at the note. "You'll have to ask her. She made a point not to tell me." She was enjoying working with Benson a lot more than having Rhonda breathing down her neck. Even if Rhonda had never assaulted her coffee.

"Interesting." Benson tucked the note into his pocket. "You watched all the videos. What's your read on this guy? The witness testimonies weren't much help. They were so shaken up, they couldn't even fully describe the clown mask he used. All of them admitted they were so focused on bagging the money, they only looked up when they heard something else crash."

"That might have been why he did it. To scare everyone and keep them jumping. There's no audio, and he was wearing a mask so you can't see his mouth move to know if he was talking."

"Do you think it was someone experienced?"

Rebecca recognized the keen way Benson watched her, waiting for her reaction. Her mouth twisted. "That's a question I don't have an answer for. I mean, why beat Carson? Why shoot him?"

"The office was the first place we were able to finish." Benson sat forward in his chair and motioned to her monitor. "We didn't find anything to suggest why Carson was attacked. The tellers couldn't hear anything in the bathroom until the gunshot. The vault between the two locations might have muffled any sounds coming from Carson's office."

Rebecca tucked a loose hair behind her ear. "Doctors report that Carson is still sedated. They're not sure when he'll be able to give a statement. His elderly mother has been brought in as his next of kin to make medical decisions for him."

"I'll keep forensics working on this. You were right, there's a lot to go through. It's going to take forever."

"If there's one thing the FBI has always excelled at, it's sorting evidence." And with the evidence in FBI lockup, she didn't have to worry about it suddenly disappearing. Which had happened with some of Wallace's evidence while waiting for trial in district court. So far, none of her evidence had gone missing. But that hadn't stopped her from making extra copies of everything.

Benson chuckled and stood, stretching his long legs. "That we are. It helps when I can call on a couple dozen more agents to come and help. If you hear anything back on that BOLO, let me know. I'm going to head back to the bank. There's only one robber to find, and we already have his plates. Maybe this'll wrap up soon."

Rebecca wasn't looking forward to Benson's departure. When she'd left the FBI, she hadn't only left her career behind. She'd also lost touch with a lot of friends and coworkers she'd grown close to over the years. Benson's presence reminded her of that.

"We should grab dinner tonight."

"You bet. Let's see how things play out today." Benson was about to say something else when Rebecca's intercom interrupted him. Elliot's voice came through.

"Sheriff, you've got a call on line one. They said it's personal, and it sounds important."

11

Not waiting for Rebecca to ask, Benson immediately left her office. Rebecca picked up the phone. "This is Sheriff West." Elliot had said it was a personal call, but she'd gotten so used to answering her phone that way that it popped out before she could think about it.

"Sheriff West, this is Deborah Niece of Shadow Homes Realty."

"How are you doing? Is everything okay? Elliot said this was personal but didn't explain."

"I'm fine, thank you for asking. That's so sweet of you. I'm recovering from the shock of Natalie's death fairly well. Uh, I'm sorry to bother you at work. I'm sure you're busy, and this isn't terribly urgent."

There was a pause, so Rebecca urged the realtor to continue. "It's okay. What can I help you with?"

"I wanted to let you know of some developments with Sand Dollar Shores. We finally have a name for the buyer. Initially, the offer came through a lawyer representing the gentleman. But Mrs. Shuping insisted on speaking with the buyer. She wanted to get a sense for the man who offered to buy her house when it wasn't even listed. Said it all felt off to her."

"Is it someone I know?"

"I don't believe so. The man who put in the offer is Claude Bennet. He owns an import-export business out of Suffolk, Virginia. He's got a personal fortune worth several million."

"Well, that explains how he could put in such a ridiculous offer."

"Yes, nearly double what it's worth."

"Did you call to tell me Mrs. Shuping accepted Mr. Bennet's offer?"

"No. Mrs. Shuping decided to post the listing to make sure everything stays above board. Neither Mr. Bennet's offer, nor the one you made before that through Ryker, were solicited, technically speaking. And I'm afraid people were whispering in her ear, telling her you might be trying to do something underhanded by buying a house from an elderly lady through back-channel deals and not in the open."

The shock at those words caused Rebecca to go rigid. "Underhanded?" She spluttered, trying to wrap her mind around that accusation. "I'm just trying to keep my house."

"I know. And Mrs. Shuping doesn't think you're doing anything wrong. But she is concerned about appearances, as much for you as for her."

Would Rebecca need to move? Would she never be able to laze on that weather-beaten porch again? She'd had a moment of pain and loss upon learning that Mrs. Shuping had nearly lost the house due to a back-taxes scheme that wasn't even legitimate. The landlady had been so shaken, she'd started talking about selling the place, which was when Rebecca offered to buy it. Now the solution to that problem might end up taking it away from her forever.

And it had to happen when she was right in the middle of

working with the FBI. She didn't need an extra reminder of everything she no longer had. That blue jacket Stalwart wore everywhere had once been her uniform—her pride and joy. She wasn't materialistic, but the few things she did have meant a lot to her.

Until today, she'd been certain her beach cottage would be the home where all those memories would be kept safe. And where more would be made.

Rebecca's heart clenched. Her emotions were all over the place. That house was her last physical connection to her parents. When she was a kid, they'd rented that house every year, and she'd grown to love the town because of it. After her parents' murders and tracking down the men responsible, she'd come back to Shadow Island to recover and heal. Instead, she'd been submersed in the fight between locals and the Yacht Club.

Losing the rental would mean scrambling for housing. If Rebecca lost the house, Ryker would have to go back to his own place. Thinking that made her feel guilty. She didn't even know his favorite movie, and he was living with her. Had they moved too fast?

The silence on the line made her realize that Deborah was waiting for her to say something. "Mrs. Shuping would have to be insane not to accept his offer. I'm aware her financial situation isn't great. With a cash offer that large, she'd be set for the rest of her life. Her money concerns would be over."

Rebecca leaned back in her chair, aware that the right thing to do was to let Mrs. Shuping sell for the higher amount. "Am I going to need to find a new place within thirty days?"

"Maybe, but she's a bit weirded out by all this. Honestly, she's worried someone might have accessed her bank accounts. While it *is* island scuttlebutt that she isn't well off, she finds the timing of this offer suspicious."

"Why is someone so wealthy trying to buy Sand Dollar Shores? Wouldn't he fit in better with those people at Sunrise Terrace?"

"That's what I thought too. He wasn't interested in any other property, saying he wanted a cozy place on the beach."

"Not too unusual. Most people who move to an island would want a beachfront home, I imagine."

"Yeah. But that's about the only part of this that isn't strange. Mrs. Shuping wants me to investigate this more before she accepts his offer." There was a pause, and Rebecca heard her landlady's voice in the background.

"She says she knows that exporting is often used as a cover for smugglers, and she doesn't want to sell to a crook when there's a sheriff who wants the house instead. I'll find a way to stall the sale, legally, of course, until we can look into this more. There's plenty of work to do. Paperwork is always a good excuse, you know."

There'd been three piles of papers waiting for Rebecca's attention, and she'd already finished one. "Yeah, it's a good excuse." She'd need to get through that paperwork before she could investigate her new housing problem.

"I've got another home that might suit him better, which I recently got a contract for. It's the Longfellow property, but I haven't had a chance to go over and do the initial walk-through or take pictures for the listing. Maybe if I get that done, I can distract him with that. It's also fully furnished. The market is super cutthroat right now. Maybe he's hoping to get a house ready to move into, and that's one of the reasons he focused on Sand Dollar Shores."

"The Longfellows are selling their house?" It was good to know Mitchell Longfellow wouldn't be coming back from wherever he'd vanished. He'd been the one whose "mistake" raised the property taxes on the house Rebecca was renting. His actions, which she was sure had been intentional, had almost led to the house being seized for back taxes.

Deborah gave a tiny laugh that sounded a bit guilty. "Yes, his wife Brittney called me. I had to fudge the truth with her a little bit. I said I'd get it all done today, but with this to deal with, there's no way I can get over there."

"Oh, I understand that. There's always something that comes up, isn't there?"

"Even on the easiest jobs."

"Thanks for letting me know. And thank Mrs. Shuping for hesitating. I appreciate it." Rebecca tried to wrap her mind around the latest complication. The position of sheriff didn't require her to be a resident of Shadow Island, but she did need to list a physical address in the county.

If she lost Sand Dollar Shores, she might not meet the requirements to run for reelection unless she could secure a replacement residence quickly. She guessed Ryker would offer his place, but she wanted time to strengthen their relationship, not put more strain on it.

"Sounds like you just got some bad news."

Startled, Rebecca turned to where Benson was standing in the doorway. Stalwart waited behind him, unease written in his posture. "Yeah. I was trying to buy a house, but I got outbid. Really, really outbid." That was downplaying it, but it wasn't a lie.

"By whom?" Benson's expression was as deadpan as ever, so she had no idea why he was asking.

She shrugged. "His name is Claude Bennet. An importer from Suffolk. Why?"

"Because with everything that's been happening, it's too convenient that someone is trying so hard to buy a house the sheriff happens to be interested in. I'll have Stalwart look into this." Benson tucked his note into his jacket.

Knowing someone else thought it was suspicious was reassuring. "I can't believe it either. Which means it probably isn't a coincidence."

12

From his vantage point in the bullpen, Hoyt couldn't help but overhear the conversation between his boss and the Special Agent in Charge. He scowled and raked his hand through his hair before jamming his hat back on tight. Benson was right. Houses on Shadow Island simply didn't sell that fast. Not only that, there was an unspoken rule on the island. Locals sold to locals first.

If Rebecca was trying to buy a house and some investor came in wanting the same house, she should get first dibs. Of course, none of those unwritten rules were legally binding.

He rapped his knuckles on the doorframe of Rebecca's office, giving the agent a nod as the other man walked out. "Hey, Boss. If you're having problems with your housing, I know a couple of folks who are searching for someone to rent their places 'til spring. You want me to get their numbers for you?"

"Uh, you heard all that, then? I appreciate the offer, but Deb is already helping me out. And I can always grab another rental place or even a room at the motel if push comes to shove." Rebecca sighed and dropped her face into her hands, rubbing her temples. She clearly wasn't happy.

Hoyt knew what that house meant to her. Everyone did. It was the reason she was here in the first place, and the reason she ended up becoming their sheriff.

"Well, yeah, and Deborah's great at her job. But one of the perks of a small town is knowing someone who has precisely what you need when you need it. We all help each other out around here."

"Yes, and while I appreciate that, I don't want to give the impression of improperly benefitting from something like that."

Hoyt slipped into her office, closing the door behind him, and sat down in his usual place, propping his feet up on the box of paper he used as a footstool. "Aw, no one would think that. This is how we all look out for each other. Everyone does it for everyone else. You're going to have to get used to it."

"Okay. Better to have too many options than not enough." She eyed the closed door. "I'm guessing you're not here just to talk to me about rentals. So what's up?"

Suddenly, he was rethinking his decision to talk to her. She already had so much on her plate. "Maybe this is a bad time to bring it up…" He bent his knees, ready to drop his feet down from the footstool so he could leave her alone.

She waved a hand, motioning him to stay seated. "Spill it. I'd rather deal with things as they happen than let them fester and grow worse. Even if I can't do anything about it now, I can still think it through before it becomes pressing."

This was certainly an issue that could turn bad fast if it wasn't taken care of. "You know how Locke was acting kind of weird yesterday?" He waited for her to nod. "I asked around a bit. He's been taking a lot of flak in town from his so-called friends. They've been showing up around his house, harassing him. Even going so far as to use juvenile bullying tactics so he no longer feels comfortable in the places he's used to frequenting."

"What are they doing?" Rebecca laced her fingers together and rested her chin on the back of them.

He'd seen the same look once in a street cat's eyes as it stared at a chunk of bread on the beach. Moments later, an unsuspecting hungry seagull had its neck bit through by the patient cat because it made the mistake of diving for its meal. He took a moment to make a mental list of the things the man-babies in the Aqua Mafia were doing to the inexperienced deputy.

"Accidentally spilling drinks on him at bars. Then throwing money at him to pay for new clothes. Someone posted an ad on Facebook saying to call his number and do your best pig call for a chance to win a prize. They had a pig delivered to his house too. It was a present, they said. Bags of garbage have been left on his Charger or under the tires. One of them backed into his car and left a long scratch down the side."

"And let me guess, either paid to have it fixed or handed over their insurance information." Rebecca's tone held a level of disgust that was usually saved for talking about boneheaded adventures of idiot teenage boys, not grown men, so Hoyt was certain she understood what was happening.

"You got it in one. Not one of the things they're doing is technically a crime, since every time they mess something up, they offer reimbursement and he accepts it."

"But it *is* harassment. He's a forty-one-year-old deputy and they're treating him like a middle schooler. It's ridiculous. Have him document every incident and ask if he'll allow us to pull his phone records for proof. I'll put the case together myself, so he doesn't have to worry about it."

Hoyt knew that if she did that, they'd accuse him of running to his mommy to complain.

"And when they try to taunt him about running to his mommy or whatever, I'll ask them if they want me to call their daddies or their daddies' lawyers to try and get them out of trouble again because they only get the one call." Rebecca wore a look of satisfaction on her face, as if she were eager to have that conversation with them.

It was like she'd read his mind, and she laughed as she caught him with his jaw hanging open.

"I worked on The Hill. At least seventy-five percent of the so-called 'men' up there are exactly like those cowards. Rich, pampered princes, some with gray hairs, who want to seem tough while having the emotional and social maturity of a playground bully."

The people Hoyt was talking about were in their thirties and forties, but their actions were so childish, it was hard not to think of them as adolescents. "I'll talk to him and see what he says. We'll also need to get all their names." He prepared to leave but stopped when he saw her watching him with a knowing eye.

"What else is bothering you?"

Hoyt sighed. Rebecca could read anyone's expression. He'd come to believe it was a superpower. "He was still here when I came in this morning. He said he was researching something on his computer, but then he also claimed it was unimportant. Then he logged off before I could see what he was looking at. When I pressed him on it, he said he's working on a theory."

"What kind of theory?"

"He wouldn't tell me that either." He shook his head.

"I'll check the logs and see what he was digging into. If it was on the servers, I should be able to see what it was."

"You know, he no longer talks to anyone. After the rumor

about him being a gossipy hen got started." Hoyt was starting to feel like a gossiping hen himself, tattling on his fellow deputy.

Rebecca only raised an eyebrow. "Which might be more of the Aqua Mafia stooges trying to alienate him now that he isn't being their yes-man anymore. I'll set up a new patrol route to have day shift go by his house more often. We'll keep an eye on him while he's sleeping."

"I was hoping you'd say that. I already drew one up. I'll send it to you."

Hoyt was glad Rebecca was taking this seriously. Locke had worked hard since the Lovecraft case to get himself on the right track. It would be a shame to see a man who was trying to turn his life around get pushed down the wrong path again.

13

Rebecca was finishing her last stack of paperwork when her phone rang—her direct line, not a transfer from dispatch. "Sheriff West speaking, how can I help you?"

"You can tell me a good place to eat in your town. Then maybe even meet me there?" Benson's words shook her out of her paperwork stupor. Doing a complete remodel of the station required a ridiculous amount of documentation. Her brain felt like mush inside her head. It was after five already, and her stomach growled at the mere mention of food.

"Seabreeze Café. One street down from the bridge, on the way to the station. Betty serves the best shakes in the world and the juiciest club sandwich you've ever had." Her stomach growled again. "I'd be more than happy to meet you there. Say in fifteen minutes?"

"Sounds good. I asked Stalwart, but he's off on a digital trail. We won't hear from him again until he's done or we forcefully remove him from his keyboard."

That sounded promising. "Is the investigation going well, then? Do you have anything to tell me yet? Are you going to hand it over to us?"

"I'm not sure. We can discuss it at dinner. I haven't eaten since an early breakfast this morning. Why don't you go ahead and invite that boyfriend of yours too?"

Rebecca shot Ryker a message. He'd been cleared to drive again. But something had come up on his last checkup, and they wanted him to continue being observed, even though he was no longer taking strong anti-inflammatories. She thought his doctor was a little too cautious with his recovery, but Ryker seemed fine with it, so she kept her mouth shut.

"My GPS says I'm about ten minutes away. I'll meet you there."

"That works for me. I'll see you soon." Her smart phone chimed as Ryker texted her back, saying he'd join them. "And you can meet Ryker too."

"Well, hey there, Sheriff West. How ya doing? I haven't seen you in a while now." Betty, the owner, was all smiles for Rebecca as she walked in the front door of the Seabreeze Café, but her eyebrows furrowed a bit as she cocked an eye at Special Agent in Charge Benson. He was standing patiently, his hands in his pockets, against the wall of the foyer. "You eating alone again?"

"Not today, Betty." She motioned to Benson, who gave both women a nod. "This is my old friend and mentor, Special Agent in Charge Percy Benson. He came down to deal with the bank robbery."

Betty shared her welcoming smile with Benson and grabbed an extra menu and two rolls of silverware. "Well, any friend of Becca Bat's is a friend of mine. I'll take you to your usual table then."

"Ryker's going to be joining us too." Rebecca's

announcement prompted Betty to grab a third menu and set of silverware.

"I'll bring him out as soon as he gets here." Betty led them past the metal-rimmed counter and cherry-red booths, through the side door, and up to a cast-iron table with matching chairs. They passed several tables of people on the way. It was the middle of dinner rush, and the café was near capacity. At least half of the patrons paused what they were doing to greet Rebecca.

Betty spread out the menus on the table. "I'll be right back with some water and a coffee for you, hun."

Benson waited for Betty to go back inside before lifting an eyebrow. "Becca Bat?"

"That's me." She crossed her legs and leaned back in her chair with no shame at all. "I was only a little girl when I first started coming here. Betty was my favorite server, and even after all these years and probably hundreds of thousands of faces coming and going, she still remembered me when I returned to the island."

Benson grinned. "That's nice."

Rebecca's smile faded. "That's what she called me back then, and honestly, it reminds me of a simpler time, when my folks were still alive. But she's the only human being who can call me by a nickname."

"Why bat?"

"Because I carried around a red plastic baseball bat that whole first summer. One of those big fat ones, you know? I think I knocked some dishes off the table. I can't remember. Anyway, she was probably worried there was a tall dude in a suit with an unreadable face lying in wait for me."

"Is that why she was so cold to me?" He unwrapped his silverware and laid the napkin in his lap.

"Most likely. She's a very protective woman. I wouldn't want to get on her bad side, especially when all the delicious food is on her good side." Seated at the late sheriff's table, Rebecca opened her menu and pointed to the long list of milkshakes. "You're going to want to save room for one of these."

"And here I thought it had something to do with the color of my skin." Benson clasped his hands and rested them on the table.

"I'm not going to say people like that don't live here." Rebecca shrugged. "But Betty's not one of them. And she doesn't allow nonsense like that in her restaurant either. Or any other kind of bigotry."

Benson gave a short nod. "Wanted to make sure you weren't wearing rose-colored glasses. This is your childhood getaway, after all. You've told me enough times about the amazing summers you spent here as a kid. Sometimes people can't see reality through the fog of their memories. It'd be hard to do your job if you still had that same mindset."

"About most things, no. About the marshes? They're still gross, smelly, and full of snakes…and leeches, which I learned the hard way." She scowled and shook her head, trying not to give away any sign of the uncertainty that'd been sitting in the pit of her stomach all day.

Benson actually shuddered. "Let's not talk about that."

She tucked that into the back of her mind the next time she needed a prank idea.

"Fine." She glanced around. "There's been plenty to remind me this isn't the place I used to know. In fact, I'm probably going to lose the vacation house I've been renting. It's the same place my parents and I rented all those years ago. I might end up in one of the weekly rate hotels for a while."

"Wait. You mean the phone call I overheard? That conversation was about the place you're staying now, the rental?"

"The rental was going to be the 'new place.'" Rebecca gave him a quick rundown of everything that led to her making an offer to buy Sand Dollar Shores and what Deborah had told her that afternoon. "If Mrs. Shuping takes the deal, and she'd be a fool not to, then I'll need to find a new place fast."

"That's the house this Bennet guy is trying to buy? Not just a random house you were hoping to get, but the specific reason you came down here in the first place?"

Rebecca nodded. "That's the one. I'd really like to know what he plans on doing with it. I can't stop him from buying it, but it'll break my heart if he plans to tear it down or something."

Earlier that day, when she told him the story of the fraudulent taxes and the landlady, Benson just shook his head. Now he was leaning forward. "What is it about you? You always seem to find yourself in the most complicated situations."

Rebecca laughed. "You have no idea. I've been in it up to my neck since the day after I got here. I swear, all I wanted was a vacation to clear my head. Then the old sheriff came to my door, while I was still unpacking, mind you, and asked for help. Things snowballed until," she waved her hands out, "here we are. Now I'm trying to buy a house while living with my boyfriend who's recovering from a traumatic brain injury that was caused by one of my many creepy cases."

Benson scratched his five o'clock shadow, which was growing in as gray as his hair. "He's moved in already, that's right. You said that. You really are in the deep end and sinking fast." He laughed out loud and was still laughing when Betty arrived with a tray of drinks.

"That's the kind of thing I like to hear in my place. Talking about falling in love and sinking fast. It's always a worry when you have two law enforcement people having a chat."

"No gross stuff at the table. I know the rule, Betty. No worries." Rebecca took the cup of coffee from the older woman.

"I didn't bring any gross stuff with me." Benson took a glass of ice water and smiled at Betty, who beamed back at him. "I'm not planning to talk shop either. Just hoping to enjoy a relaxing dinner with an old friend while I'm off the clock."

"Evening, Sheriff!"

Rebecca glanced up at the couple walking down the sidewalk and waved, waiting to see if they were going to come over to talk. Emboldened by her expression, the woman walked over.

"Sheriff, can you tell us when Dee's will be open again?"

"It should be soon. Dee said the inspector was coming out sometime this week to do the final check on the new planks he installed."

"Oh, that's great news!" The woman moved back to the sidewalk where the man was waiting for her. "Thanks for letting us know."

Rebecca waved again before turning back to Benson. Betty, used to such events, had taken Benson's drink order and gone back inside. Before they could pick up where they'd left off, another man called out from across the street.

"Heya, Sheriff. Did you hear Pastor Brett is holding a clothing drive this weekend?"

"I didn't. Thanks for letting me know. I'll spread the word."

"Let everyone know. He's hoping for children's clothes, primarily."

"Will do." Rebecca waved at him, then shifted her direction as Ryker's truck came into view, pulling up to a parallel parking spot on the street. "Ryker's here."

Benson turned in his seat to watch as Ryker parked,

climbed out, and stepped over the chain to join them on the patio. Considering he'd nearly died seven weeks ago, he looked good.

"Ryker Sawyer, meet Special Agent in Charge Percy Benson, an old friend and mentor of mine. Percy, this is Ryker Sawyer, handyman extraordinaire."

"Percy, good to meet you." Ryker shook his hand before giving Rebecca a peck on the temple. "How are you liking our little town? Thinking about moving here as well?" He grinned at Rebecca and pulled his chair closer so he could hold her hand while they sat.

"No, I'm perfectly happy staying inland, where there's a lot fewer storms and seagulls." Benson laughed. "Though given how the locals seem to love their sheriff, I might consider it. I've never seen a town so friendly to the head of their law enforcement."

"Yeah, it's that time of day. And Rebecca is sitting in the sheriff's seat. Everyone knows that Wallace used to sit here and answer questions for hours at a time. They seem to expect the same from her." Ryker frowned slightly and shook his head.

"And you don't approve?" Benson glanced at Rebecca.

She managed not to roll her eyes but couldn't keep the annoyance out of her expression. This was something they'd discussed before and didn't agree on.

"Not really. I think she should forge her own traditions. Following in the footsteps of the last sheriff isn't the best way to make yourself stand out. And Rebecca needs to stand out if she's going to win the election in November." Ryker squeezed her hand. "And Shadow Island needs a strong woman like her to keep us all safe."

"She's not going to win."

The voice belonged to a man walking up the sidewalk. To add to Rebecca's growing annoyance, she recognized him as

Nathan Warner, the owner of the Sunrise Cove Motel. During their several interactions, Warner had never failed to express his dislike for Rebecca.

He stopped barely on the other side of the chain barrier that separated the patio dining area from the public walkway. His sweat-soaked shirt was stretched tight around a protruding potbelly, and he was breathing heavily. It was as if the man had sprinted over for the sole purpose of harassing her. The scowl he directed at her made his small eyes nearly disappear.

"Not with the way crime has risen nonstop since she took over. We went from maybe one death a year to back-to-back bodies ever since she got here."

Ryker glared at Nathan but didn't say a word to defend her. And honestly, Rebecca didn't blame him. Nathan was a nuisance with a big mouth and a small brain. He said the most ridiculous things as a matter of course. And recently, his ire seemed to be focused on Rebecca.

Just to be safe, Rebecca tapped the pen in her pocket, setting it to record.

Seeing no resistance, Nathan took a step closer. He tugged his faded ballcap down firmly over his gray hair and took a deep breath. Apparently, he was just getting started. "She shouldn't even be sitting in that chair. Not a local, not duly elected, and despite all her highfalutin training with the FBI, she can't hold a candle to Wallace. She's not even half the man Sheriff Wallace was."

Talking sense to Nathan had never worked, but Hoyt had clued her in that talking nonsense to him was a good way to chase him off. Rebecca looked down at herself and patted her flat stomach. "I'll admit, I don't have Wallace's build, but isn't it a bit rude to comment on a dead man's weight?"

Benson laughed, and Ryker dropped his head, hiding his own smile at the quip.

Straightening a little, Benson turned to Nathan. "I can assure you, if you'll take the word of someone who helped her get that highfalutin FBI training, that Sheriff West is qualified for this position. As for her being duly elected, once a sheriff dies, quits, or otherwise becomes incapable of performing their sworn duties, it is up to the county officials to appoint a new sheriff or to schedule a special election."

Nathan opened his mouth. "I—"

"Your officials chose to ratify her as the sheriff." Benson gestured to Rebecca but kept his gaze fixed on the nuisance. "If you don't like that, take it up with them."

Nathan pulled his head back sharply, causing his jowls to shake. "You're not from around here. What makes you think you know any better than us locals do about how we should elect our sheriff?"

Benson shrugged casually. "I'm not from here, no. But I do know how to read county bylaws and ordinances. They're on the Dare County government website. You should read them. That was the first thing I did when I got a complaint forwarded to me about an FBI special agent posing as a county sheriff here. So again, I can assure you that Sheriff West is a duly appointed and sworn sheriff for this county."

"That doesn't change the fact that crime has only gotten worse since she swooped in and took over." As per his usual modus operandi, Nathan ignored facts and simply raised his voice, attracting the attention of other people on the street. From behind Rebecca, murmuring started at the occupied tables. Gossip would spread, and she wouldn't let Nathan's words be the last.

"Sadly, crime has gone up. I doubt it has anything to do with my being here and more to do with Wallace being killed on the job."

Rebecca twisted in her seat to face Nathan where he stood on the sidewalk. Doing so also allowed her to keep a peripheral view on the rest of the diners on the patio while still recording their interaction. She lifted her chin so she could project her voice and be heard by anyone nearby.

"After Wallace was killed, Deputy Locke and I arrested the Yacht Club's hired hands who shot him while attempting to transport an underage girl to one of their party yachts for unknown reasons." Though the incident was common knowledge, Rebecca left out the details. Everyone had heard the sad story of Cassie Leigh, the teenager who had an affair with her boyfriend's married father. After finding out Cassie was pregnant, the father murdered her.

"It's obvious the Yacht Club bosses didn't like me arresting three of their stooges. They probably liked it even less when I broke up that child trafficking ring a week later. I know that because they threatened Deputy Frost and me when they felt I wasn't investigating the retribution murders of their members enthusiastically enough."

Nathan looked ill. "I—"

"The Yacht Club really didn't like it when I continued to do my job and stopped illegal property sales, like the one involving the historic lighthouse. Deals that would only pad their already fat wallets. Because I didn't cave to political pressure after that, the Aqua Mafia has continued to try and chase me out of town."

She turned her head slowly, taking in every face, every citizen who was listening.

"We all know why crime has gone up since I became sheriff. And anyone who says they don't know why is only fooling themselves. It was the brave teens and young adults of this town who explained to me who and what the Yacht Club was."

Rebecca sat a little taller in Wallace's old seat.

"Yacht Club is too legit of a name for them, though. Let's call them what they are. They're the Aqua Mafia, a gang of wannabe mafiosos. But they're United States citizens and, as such, are constrained by the same laws as you and I are, Nathan. As sheriff, it's my duty and privilege to make sure those people are arrested and face their day in court."

A small crowd formed as people from inside the restaurant and down the street came closer, drawn over by Nathan's loud rants. But now they listened to Rebecca. Some looked confused and others looked angry, but most seemed hopeful.

"It would go faster if people who had information on the gang's illegal activities would come forward. But I can understand why some people don't. We won't stop until those responsible for Wallace's death have their day in court."

Nathan seemed to be in shock, his tongue flapping like a dying fish. A few people called out praises for Rebecca, but she kept her focus on Nathan.

"If any of you have information that can help, you can call and leave an anonymous tip. It can be about suspected Aqua Mafia members or to report suspicious or outright criminal activity. You can also tell me if you just don't like them."

Rebecca's lips twisted up slightly as Nathan jerked back. He opened his mouth once again before giving up and storming back the way he had come.

"Or if you want an extra layer of protection, you can always call the FBI tip hotline at one-eight-hundred-call-FBI or go to our website, tips dot FBI dot gov." Benson also projected his voice loud enough to be heard by everyone.

Rebecca gave Benson a nod of thanks and for the first time noticed how uncomfortable Ryker was. He'd angled away from her and let go of her hand at some point during her speech. She'd never hidden her attempts to take down the Yacht Club, but she'd never said it out loud in public before either.

For a moment, she worried about Ryker's safety. While he

was living with her, he was as much a target as she was. Seeing his deeply furrowed eyebrows, she feared she'd gone too far and put them both in danger.

While Rebecca wasn't afraid for her own safety, she couldn't help but worry about his, especially since he was still recovering from the last attempt on her life.

14

"Are you going to tell me what has you so grumpy this morning?" Rebecca asked Ryker after he'd slammed the third cupboard door while putting away his breakfast fixings. On days she had off, they'd normally spend a leisurely morning together and make a large breakfast.

Today, though, Ryker had woken up after she'd taken Humphrey on his morning run. When she'd asked about it, he'd claimed he didn't want to wait for her and had a bowl of cereal instead.

His chief complaint was generally that she worked too much, but she'd been home on time the last few nights. And it was all thanks to Benson and his team handling the bank robbery. Having that many Feds driving around town had a quieting effect on criminals. Even the normal complaints over petty issues had slacked off.

Ryker shook his head and stormed off to her bedroom, slamming that door too.

Since last night, he'd been in a bad mood. She couldn't understand why. He'd claimed it was a headache after a stressful day, but he hadn't even pretended to protest when she offered to sleep in the spare room so he could recover. Personal space and quiet time often cured his funks, and she didn't mind giving him that. But she hated being chased out of her own room.

Rebecca's generosity had its limits. If Ryker was still acting this way when she got home tonight, he could do so in the spare room while she slept in her own bed. She wasn't used to living with a significant other and had never thought it would be like this.

Rebecca grabbed her own breakfast, reheated leftovers from Seabreeze Café, and took them onto the back patio with her cup of coffee. Humphrey rushed over as soon as she took her first step to the door, his entire body wiggling at the prospect of going out again.

They'd been working on basic commands, so she told him to wait while she opened the door. She set her food on the table, bracing it just in case.

"Okay, Humphrey, go play."

Humphrey bolted out the door, still wiggling, and bounced off the patio table in his excitement. Her fork skittered around on her plate but didn't fall. She sipped her coffee and stood watching the chocolate Lab bound into the sand, sniffing everything as if he hadn't just been outside a few minutes ago.

He'd finally learned the recall command and had been deemed reliable enough to roam the yard on his own with only slight supervision. Rebecca sat down to eat her club sandwich. The fries weren't nearly as good after being reheated in the toaster oven, but it was better than letting them go to waste. Reheated leftovers had been standard breakfast fare before Ryker moved in.

"I guess the honeymoon phase is over." She grumbled into her cup of coffee as she watched Humphrey shove his nose into the sand before sneezing it out. He shook his head and decided it would be safer to sniff the dune grasses instead.

The first couple of weeks after Ryker had moved in, they'd made a concerted effort to spend as much time together as possible, holding hands and cuddling on the couch. Most nights, they would sit on the deck and watch the sun set together.

But lately, things had been chaotic. Last night was the first time in a long time they'd eaten dinner together.

Maybe it was stupid of her to agree to let him move in. They'd only recently started their relationship. If not for Ryker's medical needs, there was no way she would've agreed to it. But he was a fairly easy patient, and he'd recovered enough to be cleared for everything but the most strenuous work.

Which still meant they couldn't have sex—or at least that was the one activity his doctor had specifically forbidden, for now.

Rebecca mulled that over as she glanced at her bedroom window. Though the light was on, she could hardly make out his shape through the sheer curtains. She thought he might have been pacing while talking on the phone, but that was just a guess.

That *could* be the reason she was so sensitive and on edge. Lying next to the man she loved and not being able to be intimate was a unique kind of torture, one she'd been enduring for more than a month. They hadn't been together since before the shootout on Little Quell Island that had ended with them both in the hospital recovering from serious wounds.

And it wasn't like they were really living together. Ryker had his own home still, and now he was driving on his own too. More than a week had passed since the last time his short-term memory fritzed on him, which was the reason he'd needed someone to stay with in the first place.

If he went back to his house, and they could both have their privacy and personal space again, maybe they could go back to how they'd been before. Or was this a sign they weren't compatible and she should simply let things fade away?

She bit into the corner of her sandwich triangle, grumpy that she didn't have anyone she could call and talk to about this. Then she snorted with laughter at the absurdity of that. Viviane loved gossip. She would be over in a hot second if she thought Rebecca needed her. In fact, so would Vi's mother, Meg.

Thinking about them made her realize she could also call Rhonda if she wanted to discuss "boy problems." If she was wanting someone to vent to, she could call up Kelly Hunt, Angie Frost, Bailey Flynn, or even Pastor Brett.

All of them had made it clear through their actions that they considered Rebecca a friend. They'd already each offered her a supporting shoulder and willing ear. She smiled, then lost it as the back door swung open.

"I'm sorry I've been such an ass." Ryker plopped down in his chair and reached out to take her hand.

Rebecca squeezed the fingers wrapped around hers. "We all have bad days. Do you want to talk about it?"

Ryker stared into her eyes, and she braced herself for whatever he was about to say.

"You scared the crap out of me last night. You can't keep calling the Yacht Club the Aqua Mafia."

Rebecca was startled. That was not what she'd been expecting. Ryker had made a face when she sparred with Nathan but hadn't said anything at the time. She started to pull her hand out of his but stopped when he held her tighter.

"It took me this whole time to understand why. And to understand why I was so angry when I realized you'd gone out with Humphrey to go for a run this morning before I got up." He took a deep breath. "You didn't only call out the Yacht Club last night. You threw down a gauntlet and mocked them. These aren't the kind of people you can just humiliate and expect to get away with it, Rebecca."

She frowned. Ryker's fear was understandable. Especially after all they'd done and how much he supported her. Hell, he'd been one of the first people on the island to tell her about the Yacht Club. At the time, he hadn't seemed to think they were that big of a deal. His stance on that had barely changed since then. Why was he now so worried about them?

Oh. Because now he knows how far they'll go and what they're willing to do.

"I'm scared, and I overreacted. I'm sorry. They've already killed one sheriff. And you publicly stated how you were going to war with them." He held a hand up as if to stop her from disagreeing, and she let him spill it all. "I know it was mostly to get people on your side and to fight back against what Nathan was saying."

That last part wasn't true, but the first part was so endearing, she let it go.

"I didn't realize it would affect you this much. The Yacht Club," she refrained from saying Aqua Mafia so as not to upset him, "needs to know I won't back down. They can't traffic teenage girls. They can't run drugs in these waters. But I will do my damnedest to make sure you're not caught in the crossfire. I'd understand if you want to take a break until all this is settled."

"Never." His thumb slid over the back of her hand. "I'll have your back whatever happens."

15

Hoyt Frost dropped into his seat and jiggled the mouse on his desk to wake up the computer. It was a fabulous early fall day with perfect weather. The sun was shining and the wind held a hint of chill, a reminder of the cooler temps that would come in the next couple of weeks. This was one of those perfect days where all he wanted to do was sit in his boat, watch his fishing line, and sip beers while chatting with friends.

Instead, he'd only just gotten back from his patrol, which took him to Locke's neighborhood. Locke lived in his mom's old house, which he inherited when she died from a heart attack seven years ago. Locke had never moved on. The place was shut up against the morning sun, which made sense, considering he worked nights. Nothing else had looked out of place. Maybe the patrols were working.

"You just get back from Trent's place?" Viviane set a cup of coffee on Hoyt's desk.

He glanced up at her and shrugged. "Yep. Everything seems fine over that way."

She gave a tiny nod of acknowledgment and went to sit and savor her own cup of coffee. "That's good."

"When'd you start calling him Trent?"

Viviane tapped her bottom lip as she thought about it. "I'm not sure really. Recently, I guess. He's become a lot more personable." She shrugged as if it didn't matter and turned to her computer.

"Less of a prickly douchebag, you mean."

"That too."

Hoyt sipped his coffee, thinking about how far the man had come. For the first time, he realized he'd never really treated him like a colleague. From day one, Locke had been assigned the night shift. That had kept him away from the rest of the team, for the most part. He'd never participated in any of the social gatherings they did as a team either.

A large part of that was due to his work hours. Another part was his preference to hang out with his own friends. But now that those friends had turned on him, who was he socializing with? If Locke was ever going to feel loyal to the sheriff and his coworkers without succumbing to the pressure the Aqua Mafia man-babies were putting on him, he'd need support. To feel accepted and connected.

As senior deputy, Hoyt felt he should do something about that. It struck him then that he'd never taken Locke out to dinner.

He'd done that with every other coworker, at least once. Only last week, he'd taken Jake to dinner to get to know him a bit better and show him around their town. But even after six years of working together, he'd never once sat down and had a meal with Locke.

That was something he needed to fix as soon as he could.

"Well, hey, Boss. I thought today was your day off."

Viviane's greeting snapped Hoyt out of his musings, and

he lifted his gaze to see Rebecca, in uniform, walking into the bullpen.

"You really don't know how to take a break, do you?" Hoyt sighed theatrically and reached for his phone. "I'll call Angie and see if she can drag you out to the beach or something. Maybe set up a puppy playdate with Humphrey and Boomer."

Rebecca's eyes lit up at that, but she shook her head. "SAC Benson called and asked me to meet him here. He's got news for us." She walked past the rows of desks to the coffee station. "But I do like the idea of a doggy playdate. Humphrey has so much energy, it'd be nice to deflect it onto someone else every now and then."

"Does it have something to do with Stalwart?" Hoyt held up the note that had been left on his desk. "Locke said Stalwart was in the office all night, working on his laptop. That Fed was squirrely as hell the first time he came down. He's even worse now. Lurking around, not talking to anyone, keeping his nose buried in his laptop."

"If Stalwart locked up on his way out of the building and only used his own device and none of ours, I'm fine with it." Rebecca moved Greg's seat out and plopped down in it. "And if his nose is buried in his work, then he's not out in the field screwing things up. Considering how good he is at being an analyst, I say that's a win-win."

The buzzer announcing that someone was being let into the bullpen echoed through the room. Hoyt glanced over as Benson walked in.

"Sorry, West. We're not going to be handing this case over to you. I'm not kicking you off the case, but we're keeping the lead on this."

"Oh, you found something?" Rebecca sat forward.

He waved a manila case folder at her. "We found the car. It took a while. A private towing company employed by some businesses that share a parking lot towed the car for being parked in a two-hour parking spot too long. One of my team did a routine check this morning of tow yards and found it." Benson gave Rebecca a look, as if he were waiting for her to say something.

"Parked too long in a timed spot? Sounds like someone was in a hurry and a real rookie too. Either that, or he wanted to get caught. Who's the car registered to?"

Hoyt opened the case file on his computer while they were talking. "It's a rental car."

Benson nodded. "Out of Coastal Ridge. My people already called and asked about it. It was rented by a Dillon Miller."

Startled, Hoyt turned to Rebecca, who raised an eyebrow.

Rebecca shook her head in denial. "*Our* Dillon Miller? Cassie Leigh's betrayed boyfriend? He couldn't have rented a car. He's not even eighteen. Don't you have to be twenty-one to rent a car?"

Hoyt didn't blame Rebecca. He was skeptical too. "This doesn't make sense."

"If our Dillon wanted to rent a car, he'd have to use a fake ID. Who gets a fake ID with his own name on it to rent a car, then uses that car to commit a felony? What's the ID description say?"

It was hard to imagine a sweet kid like Dillon robbing a bank, let alone nearly killing a man. After having his heart broken by his past girlfriend and being betrayed by his father, the kid now kept a low profile.

Benson flipped his folder open. "Dillon Miller. Six-four. One hundred and ninety-five pounds. Brown hair. Brown eyes. And that matches the CCTV footage, by the way. Saw it myself."

"Actually," Viviane had been tapping away at her

computer as well and lifted her head, "Dillon turned eighteen last month. He's no longer a minor."

"The height matches the description of the robber too." Rebecca's eyebrows knitted together.

"We have more research to do, but this doesn't look good for Dillon Miller." Benson's words twisted Hoyt's stomach.

He didn't believe for a second that Dillon Miller could commit such a crime. But that didn't seem to matter.

16

Rebecca pulled up in front of the Miller house, close to where Dillon's basketball hoop stood near the end of the driveway. The yard was maintained, and the windows were open to the midday breeze. She'd managed to talk Benson out of joining her by explaining her history with the family and how they'd likely clam up if the FBI appeared at their door.

Owen Miller had betrayed everyone in his family long before killing his teen lover and shattering his son's heart. The poor kid had blamed the Yacht Club wholeheartedly. He'd even taken the dangerous steps of reaching out to a BC member to try to gather evidence against them and to get justice for his first love. He'd never suspected the real culprit was his own father.

His mother, Diane, had barely held it together after that. She'd completely withdrawn from everything, even her son. Considering the young man was the spitting image of his father, Rebecca could almost understand that.

Except it left a hurting and vulnerable boy to try to make his own way in the world when he most needed stability and security. Which was one of the reasons she hoped they were wrong about Dillon having rented the getaway vehicle for the bank robber.

Rebecca was skeptical that he could be the robber who'd beaten and shot the bank manager. Dillon had been so eager for justice. He'd gone above and beyond, confronting the man from the Aqua Mafia to get information and help Rebecca find a killer. There was no way that kind, sweet, moral kid could be involved in this case.

That wouldn't stop her from doing her job, though. If Dillon was innocent as she suspected, the evidence would prove that.

Rebecca got out of her cruiser and took one step before she realized where she'd parked. She and Darian Hudson had stood on the Miller's lawn discussing the Cassie Leigh murder. He'd been called away from his paternity leave with his newborn daughter, Mallory, to provide backup to an upstart ex-FBI agent with a crazy theory about a murder case.

Melancholy overtook her for a moment. She wasn't sure if it was her grief for Darian Hudson and his small family, working with Benson again, or the summer being over and the long days of winter threatening. Suddenly, she was tired.

Tired of seeing good people and good families destroyed by the influence of the Yacht Club. Tired of having to prove herself over and over again to people who only wanted to believe the worst about her. Tired of having to struggle, fight, and work grueling hours only for some rich asshole to threaten her house.

It was rich assholes who destroyed her family. Billionaire businessmen conspired with millionaire senators, not only to murder her parents but to pressure the FBI into simply letting it slide. Refusing to cave to their demands had cost Rebecca so much. Her career, reputation, old boyfriend, home, and coworkers. Not to mention the years of her life she'd devoted to taking those rich assholes down.

The psychological toll all of that had taken on her, combined with the hell her body had suffered in the last year, was more than most people would endure in a lifetime.

She'd made a good showing of herself at Seabreeze Café the other night, but dammit, she shouldn't have had to. Yes, crime had gone up, but she'd caught every bad guy involved in the serious crimes that had happened since her arrival. No one talked about that. They didn't ask her why she had a nearly one hundred percent close record on her cases.

Ryker told her that was the way things were in a small town. All gossip spread fast, but negative gossip spread the fastest. And she was running a campaign for office, which made it even worse. The entire island would be invested in how she did her job so they could make an informed decision at the ballot box.

She'd come to Shadow Island to recover, not to work harder. It was supposed to be her day off, and yet here she was, working.

Suck it up, buttercup. You can have your little pity party later. Right now, you need to make sure a young man isn't destroying his life before he even gets it started.

Rebecca pushed her shoulders back, lifted her chin, and walked up to the front door. Though she caught only a glimpse of the ocean, the gentle slap of the waves could easily be heard throughout the quiet neighborhood. That helped to calm Rebecca as she raised a fist and knocked.

Diane Miller, a pretty blond woman in her forties, answered the door after only a short wait. Her shoulder-length hair framed a face that looked years younger than the last time Rebecca had seen her. She wasn't sure if it was the new haircut or maybe a new beauty treatment, but Diane seemed to be doing much better now, even as the smile melted off her face when she saw who had knocked.

"What do you want, Sheriff?" As Diane crossed her arms, her blouse clinging tightly to her torso showed she'd gained a few pounds recently. She was no longer so thin and bony. The extra weight looked good on her.

Not sure if Diane had officially divorced her cheating, murderous ex-husband or not, Rebecca decided to forgo the honorific *Mrs.* just in case. "Afternoon, ma'am. I was wondering if I could talk to Dillon."

Diane scowled, narrowing her brown eyes. "Why?"

"Because I need to speak to him. I wouldn't trouble you if it wasn't important."

"Does this have anything to do with Cassie's murder? You already got my bastard ex-husband to confess. What could you possibly need to talk to Dillon about? He's been through enough. I don't want his recovery stunted. His therapist said it was best if he put his past behind him."

Rebecca shook her head. "No, ma'am. This is for a different case."

"A different case?" Diane pulled away. "What case?"

"That's what I'd like to talk to him about. Is he home?"

Diane straightened, her scowl fading. "No. He isn't. In fact, he's not even in the state and hasn't been for weeks now. He's in his first year of college at UNC."

Rebecca deeply hoped that was true.

"Well, that could explain it. First year students often run into scams that end up getting their identities stolen."

Diane frowned. "Do I need to be worried about that?"

"Not unless you believe he rented a car and then forgot it in a timed spot." Rebecca smiled to ease the tension. "That doesn't sound to me like something Dillon would do, which is why I need to speak to him."

"Oh, no. There's no way he'd do that." Diane eased visibly,

her eyebrows relaxing, her lips hinting at a smile. "Actually, he took his father's pickup with him. He wouldn't need to rent a car."

"Okay, well, we already have his phone number from...*before*. Do you have the address where he's staying? This is an important matter, and I'd like to get it cleared up as soon as possible." Rebecca wasn't sure what she'd said, but Diane suddenly went rigid and defensive again, grabbing the door.

"You're the police. I'm sure you can figure that out. The last time I trusted you, you destroyed our lives. I won't let you do that to my son."

Diane slammed the door so hard, the loose hairs along Rebecca's forehead blew in the wind. The whole exchange was unnervingly reminiscent of her previous encounter with Dillon's mom.

That wasn't the best way to prove Dillon's innocence, but she couldn't blame the mother. She'd been cooperative last time and, as Diane said, it had destroyed their lives. This time, if Rebecca wanted to protect Dillon, she'd have to do it without his mother's help.

17

"Yeah, thanks for all your help." Viviane snarled at the phone on her desk even though she'd already been hung up on.

"Problems, Vi?"

Viviane shot Hoyt a look. He had his head down, reading something on his computer and jotting notes down in his notepad. Seeing that he wasn't about to tease her for her temper, she calmed down. "That was the car rental place. I was trying to get them to send me a copy of the rental agreement Dillon had to fill out to get that car. The agent seemed willing at first, but then suddenly stonewalled me and insisted he could only do it with a warrant."

"Yeah, that happens a lot. People are willing to tell you things. But once it gets real enough to need documentation, they start getting antsy. Can't really blame them, though. No one wants to get in trouble at work for involving the police. Just get the warrant. That usually calms things down." He glanced at his notepad, frowned, and went back to reading.

"I guess I'll have to." Viviane groused but got up to pour a cup of coffee instead. If she was going to have to start working on forms, she needed caffeine to carry her through it. As she reached for the coffee pot, she noticed the time on the display. It was fifteen minutes after noon. And she'd skipped breakfast that morning. No wonder she was feeling run-down.

Taking her steaming coffee to her desk, she grabbed her phone and shot Rebecca a message, asking if she would mind picking up lunch on her way back to the office. While waiting for a response, she clicked on the tab for the rental agency, intending to close it now that she had the local number. Instead, something at the bottom of the page caught her eye.

Rent a Car Under Twenty-One.

She clicked on it and read the disclaimer. Then she read it again, searching for any exceptions. There were none that fit Dillon Miller.

"Hey, Frost."

"Yeah?" He didn't stop his notetaking.

"Rebecca was right. The rental agency website says they don't rent to anyone under the age of twenty-one unless they're military or government agents with orders."

That got Hoyt's attention, and he stopped what he was doing. "But we know Dillon doesn't meet those criteria."

She nodded. "I know. Do you think this could be why they suddenly became so reluctant to send over the contract? They're supposed to include a copy of the driver's license. What if they screwed up and rented it to him even though they weren't supposed to? Or he used a fake ID. That could get them in trouble, too, I suppose."

Hoyt frowned and shrugged before opening a new window on his computer and typing again. "That could be the problem. But I think it makes more sense that it isn't *our* Dillon Miller."

He turned the monitor toward her, and she got up from her chair to read the list on his screen. It was the DMV database. And the entire page was filled with Dillon Millers of all ages with addresses all over the state.

"Well, that makes a lot more sense. Dillon was such a sweetie, trying to help us with the case. And so worried about Cassie. You think it was really a coincidence that the bank robber had the same name?"

"I want to." Hoyt stared at the notes he'd been taking before looking again at the list of Dillon Millers on his computer. "But honestly, he might not be the same kid we knew this past summer. Dillon went through hell. There's no telling what that might do to a young man. Betrayed by his father. Betrayed by his girlfriend. Being accused of impregnating Cassie when he hadn't even known she was pregnant."

Viviane snorted. "By his own father, no less."

Hoyt rubbed his jaw and sighed. "Let's not forget becoming the prime suspect in his girlfriend's murder before learning his dad had been the one to cross that unforgiveable line. On top of all that, he had his reputation dragged through the mud. Maybe all of that was too much to bear."

Viviane's stomach went sour listening to everything done to Dillon when he'd been totally innocent.

"I'm honestly just tossing out theories. I don't think it's him. But as officers of the law, we have to follow every lead to where it takes us." Hoyt clicked on the tab he'd been on before. "Maybe him robbing a bank for some extra money was a reasonable plan. I've been going through his social media. He's still posting, but not the same way he used to. And nothing about what he's up to. Compared to before Cassie's death, there're a lot fewer posts. Barely one a day."

He scrolled through Dillon's social media pages as Viviane followed along over his shoulder. It was mostly pictures of himself. Not hanging out with friends. Basic selfies with depressing messages like *Woke up this morning anchored in reality* or *Out of ash, new seeds grow*. Hell, Dillon was barely even recognizable. His eyes were much older than they used to be.

Hoyt's phone rang and he answered it. Viviane kept scrolling while he talked, not really paying attention to him until he hung up.

"That was Coastal Ridge Hospital. Arthur took a turn for the worse this morning. They had to take him back into surgery and said things aren't going well. This bank robbery might have an additional charge of murder by the end of the day. I should update Benson."

"That poor man." Viviane hugged herself. "I hope Mr. Carson pulls through."

"You and me both. You know, he was the one who clued us in that the Aqua Mafia funneled their money through the Sandpiper Bank. He didn't say it outright. But he said if we got him the warrant, he'd happily show where all the international payments are going. Boss caught on to what he meant and has been working toward finding the right accounts to get warrants for."

"I didn't know that. Dammit. Two upstanding citizens. Both of them have tried in the past to help us take down the Aqua Mafia. There's no way this is a coincidence." Viviane chewed her lip, more determined than ever to find something to exonerate Dillon.

She started digging through the FBI's forensic files. There was nothing of help there, barely anything at all. They still didn't have anything to upload to the case file. Working so far from their lab was probably slowing them down.

Either that, or the robber is really good at hiding evidence. Could that have been the reason he made such a mess? To confuse the investigation?

She was about to voice her theory to Hoyt when Elliot leaned back in his chair and called out to them.

"Deputy Frost, I just got a report from Deborah Niece. She says there's someone lurking in Mitchell Longfellow's house. She sounds terrified."

18

As Hoyt pulled up to the Longfellow place, Deborah Niece waved at him from the sidewalk opposite the house. She'd been hiding in her car parked across the street and gotten out as they pulled up.

With a sigh, Hoyt got out of the cruiser. "After today, I'm going to need a tall vanilla shake from Betty." He snorted. "Screw today. After this week. I might go ahead and get two of them. With a beer chaser."

Viviane's eyes lit up. "Yum."

"Care to join me? I know you're supposed to get off an hour after me today, but something tells me I won't be clocking out on time."

"Hells yeah!"

Viviane was all cheerful grins, and Hoyt hated to have to dampen her good mood so quickly, but he nodded at Deborah, who was still cowering. "She could probably use one too."

Just like that, Viviane's happiness was wiped away, and she ran across the road to talk to Deborah. Hoyt jogged after.

"Deborah Niece? I'm Deputy Viviane Darby. You called

about a possible intruder?" Viviane took Deb's hand, turning her so she wasn't staring at the house any longer. Asking questions that could be answered in the affirmative was a great way to put people at ease.

Hoyt was glad to see she'd learned that lesson during her training.

"I did." Deborah's green eyes darted back and forth, and she swayed to the side to point with a shaky hand. "I came out here to do a walk-through. You know, assess what needed to be done and make it ready to show. But when I opened the front door and walked in, I heard someone coming in the back door. I called out, thinking maybe it was Mitchell or Brittney Longfellow. I pulled out my pepper spray, because we all know you can't be too careful nowadays."

Deborah Niece's business partner, Natalie Luptak, had been brutally murdered while completing a walk-through of a boathouse near the marshes. Hoyt didn't blame the realtor for arming herself.

"A man, I couldn't really make him out, stood in the back door. He was wearing a ski mask. I just know he was going to rob the place. He told me to 'get the hell out' and pulled a gun on me."

"The man was armed?" Hoyt's heartbeat sped up. He surveyed the street, but everything seemed quiet. Viviane had done the same, he noted with satisfaction. Without talking, they flanked Deborah. Both of them kept their eyes peeled, covering the street, which appeared empty. No one except Deborah seemed to have noticed anything conspicuous.

Deborah nodded, her eyes still scanning. "Well, I sprayed my pepper spray and ran as fast as I could back out the door. He screamed, and I'm pretty sure he stumbled out the back again. So I waited here for you with my engine running." She gestured back to her car. "I was ready to run him over if he came out this way."

"I bet you were." Hoyt admired the woman's spunk. He turned his focus to the house in question. He'd been to Longfellow's place before, and it seemed the same as the last time he was here, except for the curtains being closed tight and the door standing wide open. There were no cars in the driveway, but the three-car garage could have been full for all he knew.

Longfellow had moved on to bigger and better things, however, according to Richmond Vale, Chairman of the Select Board.

"Any chance Mitchell or Brittney is home?" Hoyt knew Brittney always summered elsewhere, but she should've been back by now.

"I don't know. Maybe. I thought I heard footsteps? But I'm not sure. I was freaked out." Deborah shook her head and shifted, putting Hoyt between her and the house with the intruder.

"Makes sense." Viviane's tone was soothing. Her sour mood seemed to have vanished with the promise of some action.

"Brittney wanted the house cleaned and put on the market as soon as possible. I was supposed to walk through it yesterday, but I got caught up in other things."

Hoyt scanned the yards of the houses behind the realtor. "I know you said the intruder was by the back door, but can you try to describe them?"

"Like I said, he had on a ski mask. Let's see, uh, he was shorter than you. I'm sorry. I just sprayed the pepper spray and ran."

"How about you head home now? We've got this, and we'll follow up with you later, okay?" Viviane guided

Deborah to the car door and opened it for her. "And be careful."

"I will. I will." Deborah bobbed her head and shot a glance at the house one last time before finally sitting in the driver's seat.

Once Deborah was safely inside her car, Hoyt gave Viviane a nod, and they crossed the street.

Viviane bit her lower lip. "I'd forgotten that psycho Lovecraftian guy had also been squatting in the boathouse when he killed Deborah's partner and defiled her body."

"Yeah." Hoyt had to work to keep the emotions out of his voice. This wasn't the time to think about dismembered heads staring in horror at their own flayed bodies.

They needed to be cautious, but not so worked up they got jumpy. It was a fine line to straddle, each and every time they encountered an unknown situation. Screwing up could end in injury or death.

Hoyt pulled his Glock as they got close to the door and waved Viviane to the side. He knew the layout of the house, at least on the first floor, so he was going to take point. Viviane arced to the side, pulling her weapon as well.

At her nod, he stepped in, pushing the door fully open against the wall before swinging his gun muzzle left to right, clearing the foyer. "Sheriff's Office. Come out with your hands up!"

There was a set of stairs leading to the second floor on the left while the rest of the house opened to his right. Viviane followed him in, her gun finding the stairs and tracing them up.

With Viviane covering the stairs, Hoyt stepped to the right and through the doorway. With his gun leading the way and his eyes constantly scanning, he stepped into the den. It was exactly the same as the last time he'd seen it. Heavy leather recliners, shelves of sports memorabilia, the flat-screen television Longfellow used for watching game show reruns.

After three more cautious steps into the room, he could see the opening that led to the kitchen. Hoyt glanced back at Viviane. She stepped up next to the door to the den, then stopped, tucking herself into the corner so she could see both the kitchen doorway and the stairs. He leaned to his right, trying to get a look farther into the kitchen.

From what he could view, it was empty. It was what he couldn't see that had him on edge.

"I've got your back."

He glanced over at Viviane. If he moved farther into the house, he'd be out of her sight. But if she moved farther to stay with him, she couldn't cover the front door and stairs. He had to trust her to know what she was doing, and she had to trust him.

Hoyt stepped into the kitchen. The tile floors had a smear of mud on them near the back door, the dead bolt latch in the unlocked position. Though the kitchen island was large, it featured open shelves with no doors, and it was empty enough that he could see through to the other side. The room was unoccupied.

Calling out what he was doing so Viviane would know would take away the element of surprise he'd need if the armed suspect was still inside. As quietly as possible, he began clearing the home.

Hoyt yanked open the door that led toward the center of the house. He twitched as he saw a man's shape before realizing he was looking in a mirror. The powder room was empty as well.

He spun around, facing the last door. It should lead to the garage, but he couldn't be certain. Four steps took him to the door, and he yanked it open.

It wasn't the garage. A top-load washer and dryer sat

along one wall. Opposite those was a wall of open hooks with a bench and storage cubbies underneath. Another door next to the coat area led to the backyard. He tried the handle, but it was locked.

One last door was on the far side of the small mudroom. Yanking the door open, he found himself staring into a vacant garage. There wasn't a car in sight, just an open expanse with a concrete floor.

"Clear!" Leaving all the doors open, Hoyt spun on his heel and moved to survey the rest of the main level. On the far side of the kitchen was a small room with no door. All four walls were lined with floor-to-ceiling bookshelves. One oversize leather chair sat in the middle with a matching leather footstool. A small side table was next to the chair.

Leaving the library, Hoyt surveyed the remainder of the first floor. There was one large great room that didn't look like it had ever been used. One couch sat against the opposite wall, and he checked to make sure no one was hiding behind it.

"All clear!" He rejoined Viviane by the front door. If there was anyone left in the house, they'd be getting anxious by now, as half the house was already checked. The only place they could be was upstairs.

Viviane was waiting, gun held steady on the staircase. Hoyt stepped up next to her and motioned for her to go first, but she shook her head. "There's a hidden door under the staircase. Take a closer look at the baseboard."

Hoyt inspected the paneling where she'd pointed. Sure enough, one panel didn't quite reach the floor, hovering less than half an inch above the tile. He stepped forward and tapped his fingers hard against the wood. It was hollow. Seeing no hinges and no handle, he made an educated guess that it would be a magnetic latch. If it was anything else, he wouldn't know how to open it anyway.

Keeping his right arm up and his gun steady, Hoyt started pressing along the top decorative strips of wood until he felt one give. When he pressed harder, the door swung away from him. His heart clenched in his chest at the sudden movement, even though he'd been expecting it.

It was a closet, stacked with luggage, winter coats, and shoes on wood shelves. To be sure, he stepped in and pushed things around, making sure no one was hiding behind the bags.

"Clear."

Viviane waited until he got back before starting up the stairs. It was always tricky going to the second floor while clearing a house. You had to check in front, above, behind, and sometimes to both sides as well. This time, the stairs were thankfully along one wall with the second floor opening up only to the right. As Viviane stepped off the final stair, she spun, covering the open area to their right.

Hoyt passed her, keeping an eye in front and to the right. Back and forth they passed each other, taking their time to clear each room.

"It's all clear." Viviane blew out a breath.

"But did you see what I saw?" Hoyt put his gun in his holster and snapped it secure.

Viviane grabbed her radio, ready to call it in. "If you mean the master bedroom with the closet rifled through and the empty bank bags on the floor, yeah, I sure did."

19

Rebecca pulled her cruiser across Mitchell Longfellow's driveway. Hoyt waved her down from his position in the front doorway, then pointed across the street. SAC Benson pulled up as well, and he had Agent Stalwart with him.

She hopped out of her SUV and crossed the street, waving for Benson to join her.

"Deborah, are you okay?" The real estate agent was pale under her tan, and she was blinking way too fast.

Before Deborah could answer, Viviane crossed the street to join them. "Why are you still here? We told you to go home."

"I couldn't let Hoyt and you handle this alone. I was ready to drive over that rat bastard if he ran out this way."

Rebecca bit back a laugh and made sure her face showed only concern.

"I'm fine. I'm fine." Deborah's messy bun flopped around as she nodded jerkily. "I'm so glad you guys came when I called. I know I had to sound like a madwoman when I was on the phone. Talking about intruders." She blew out a breath, and Rebecca reached out to hold her hand, casually resting her fingers along Deborah's wrist.

Her pulse was fast, but not too bad, and it was steady.

"Are you sure you don't want to sit down? I'm going to need you to tell me what happened again. I'm sorry, but police work is all about redundancy." She laughed, trying to put the other woman at ease.

It worked a little, and Deborah laughed with her. "Oh, I know. Everything involving the law has to have everything checked three times before you can move on to the next step." She motioned with her chin. "Who's he?"

Rebecca turned to Benson as he strode up behind her. "Deborah Niece, meet my good friend Special Agent in Charge Percy Benson with the FBI. Percy, this is Deborah Niece, who runs the Shadow Homes Real Estate Agency."

"A special agent? Like you were? Is he visiting you?" Deborah reached out to shake Benson's hand.

"Visiting yes, but also working." Benson cast aside his normal stony expression and smiled wide enough to light up his eyes. "Can't let Rebecca here be the only agent you all meet. You'd think we were all jokesters who never took our jobs seriously."

Viviane spun on Benson and looked like she was about to say something but bit her lip instead and slanted her gaze toward Rebecca.

She shook her head, smiling, letting Viviane know it was okay.

Deborah burst out laughing. "Rebecca? A jokester? Our Rebecca?" She turned to her and shook her head, bewildered. "That's a side of her I haven't seen."

"That's because you've never made me mad enough to tape an airhorn to the bottom of your desk chair." Rebecca swiveled her head around to raise her eyebrows at Benson.

Viviane clapped a hand over her lips, stifling her giggle.

"Which," Benson cut in as Deborah choked on laughter, "is not the best idea in an office filled with armed agents."

"Oh, dear!" Benson and Rebecca's banter had worked its magic, and Deborah was finally calm. Viviane, on the other hand, was going to pop a vein from holding in her laugh as she struggled to keep a professional expression on her face.

"So if you wouldn't mind, could you walk us through the house and let us know if anything is missing from inside?"

Deborah started to nod, then froze. "I can't do that." She darted a guilty glance at Rebecca. "Not that I won't. But I never came over yesterday like I was supposed to. I had a, um, special project I was working on last night. The first time I've ever been in this house was today. And I only made it to the foyer."

Rebecca realized the special project she'd been working on was the situation with Sand Dollar Shores. "I understand. Tell me what you can."

"Brittney Longfellow contacted me Sunday evening to sell the place. I told her I could get the first walk-through done Monday morning. By then, I already had that other thing to work on. And I knew this job would be a bit complicated since the house is still furnished. She said that a lot of things were left behind and wanted me to work with a moving company to clear out the personal items."

"The Longfellows still have personal items here?"

"That's what she told me."

"When are you meeting with her next to discuss this? I assumed she wants to be on hand when the movers show up. When is that scheduled?"

"I haven't." Deborah shook her head. "Met in person, that is. She emailed me over the weekend and sent the paperwork via fax. The keys were FedExed to my office when I got in Monday. She said she'd already moved out of state and wasn't planning to come back. I assumed marital trouble. But the house is solely in her name, so she can do what she wants."

"And you've already given your statement to Deputy Darby or Deputy Frost?" Rebecca glanced over at Viviane and got a nod at the same time Deborah answered.

"Yes. There wasn't much to tell. I didn't see anyone in the windows or yard. After I walked in, I heard something at the back door, like someone was coming inside or was already in the house. And I thought I heard footsteps. It just felt like someone was home…but I might be mistaken." She twisted her fingers together. "I'm sorry I'm not more help."

"Footsteps? Can you remember from where?" Deborah started to shake her head, but Rebecca held her hand out, signaling her to slow down. "Think for a moment. You've walked up to the front door. Did you use a key to unlock the door or a code?" Rebecca knew which kind of lock the door had, but she wanted to get the witness into the correct headspace.

"I used the key that was FedExed to me." Deborah nodded, cocking her head ever so slightly. "I stepped inside… I heard something shuffle. Upstairs. I headed farther into the house."

"What next?"

"The door to the backyard opened. I called out. I think I called Mitchell's name? And then the man appeared, holding a gun. Wearing a ski mask. I turned and ran and…" Deborah sucked in air, her eyes widening, and shook her head to negate herself. "No. He was coming toward me. That's when I sprayed him."

"With pepper spray." Viviane confirmed. "You can still smell it if you walk in."

"I ran out the front door. He was screaming and calling me all kinds of vile names. I heard the back door slam, even though I was halfway down the driveway."

"Can you describe him?" Rebecca tried to keep her voice as gentle as possible.

"Not really. He was covered, ski mask, black clothes. Taller than me. But I did hear more footsteps from upstairs as I was hightailing it out of there. Heavy footsteps. Far apart. I don't know how to explain it, but they sounded like a man running." Her eyes started jumping around again.

Rebecca continued letting Deb clutch onto her hand. "You think more than one person was in the house? The man in the ski mask and someone else?"

"Yes, I think so." She briefly closed her eyes and breathed in. "Also, there was a dirty plate left out, like someone had been eating earlier."

"Anything else?" Rebecca peered into her eyes but saw them go soft with resignation as the realtor shook her head. "Deborah, you've been exceptionally helpful. You acted rationally, called us immediately, and only told us what you noticed instead of making things up to try and be more helpful."

"Wish I could have done more."

Rebecca patted her on the arm and got a smile for her efforts. It was a trifle depressing how often she had to reassure people with that line. "If you can give us Brittney Longfellow's contact information, then you're free to go home or back to your office. We'll be taking over this residence, unfortunately. But we'll let you know when it can go on the market. Are you okay to drive?"

"Yeah, I'm fine now. Thanks, Rebecca." Deborah reached into her car to retrieve a cheap nylon binder that reminded Rebecca of the Trapper Keeper she'd carried in high school. Flipping it open, she removed a business card. "I wrote down all her information while I was waiting for you. Viviane said you'd probably need it."

After that, Deborah climbed into her car and drove off.

Benson and Rebecca walked across the street to where Hoyt was waiting.

"You know, with all the other nice things she uses for her work," Benson examined the heavy cardstock business card, "I'm surprised she carries that instead of a nice leather padfolio or something."

Rebecca winced at that idea. "Well, did you hear about the psycho we had down here cutting off people's heads and removing their skin?"

"I heard something about it. Why?" He gestured at Deborah's car as it moved down the street. "Was she one of his surviving victims?"

"No, but her best friend and business partner was the third victim. And the psycho used her skin as leather so he could cover his manifesto to make it into a sacred book for the Devourer. I can't blame her for not using leather now." Her lips thinned into a smile as he mouthed the name of the Lovecraftian god.

"You have a lot of interesting people down here." Benson shook his head in disbelief.

Rebecca laughed. "Let me tell you about another one then. Mitchell Longfellow, resident of this house, the AWOL treasurer of the Select Board. He disappeared right around the time my entire team was ambushed by cartel thugs. I've never been able to verify that Longfellow had anything to do with that, but his absence is suspicious."

Benson nodded. "I can see why you'd think that."

They stepped into the mini-mansion, and she gestured broadly, taking it all in. "Nor do I understand how a small-town government official could afford such luxuries. Perhaps working for an international cartel or an illegal drug ring that was run by the Yacht Club could fund this kind of lifestyle."

Hoyt moved around the two as they spoke. He eyed Rebecca as he ducked past. "Excuse me."

She acknowledged him with a nod. "Longfellow was also the one who jacked up the property tax on the house I'm renting in an attempt to seize it for back taxes. Those taxes were also illegally tacked on to my landlady's bill. She got it straightened out, but it spooked her enough that she decided to sell before the next tax assessment. And he's been out of town for all that."

"Shit." Benson shook his head and pulled his phone from his pocket. "I really want to talk to this guy now." Reading from the card, he dialed the number.

Rebecca waited in the foyer, Hoyt watching them both, as Benson disconnected without speaking. "His voicemail is full."

"Good to know it isn't only us he's dodging." Hoyt snorted. "I tried calling him for weeks after he left and never reached him. He never returned my messages either."

"Did you try calling his wife?" Benson glanced over his shoulder at Hoyt as he dialed a second number.

He shook his head. "Never had a reason to. She was out of the country at the time."

Benson's head popped up. "Hello, this is Special Agent in Charge Percy Benson of the FBI. I'm trying to reach Brittney Longfellow." He paused, then pressed the speaker button, motioning for Hoyt to close the door.

"This is she."

"Mrs. Longfellow, I'm afraid I need to inform you that your house was broken into. I'm inside it right now with Sheriff West and Deputy Frost."

"Broken into? Are you sure?" Rebecca thought she heard people speaking Spanish in the background. "It was supposed to go on the market this week. Maybe it was just someone viewing the house?"

"No, ma'am. It was your real estate agent who called us when she noticed there was an intruder, possibly two, in the house. I—"

"You said you're there with Sheriff West. Let me talk to him."

Rebecca scowled at the incorrect pronoun. "I'm here, Mrs. Longfellow. Was there something you need to ask me?"

"Thank you, Sheriff. Deputy Frost?" Brittney was speaking fast with a clipped tone, as if she was running a business meeting roll call.

"Yes, ma'am?" Hoyt stepped forward,

"What was the prom theme for your junior year?"

"Ma'am?" He glanced at Rebecca, perplexed. She shrugged and motioned for him to answer. "Uh, it was beach loving."

"I think you mean summer love."

The senior deputy shrugged. "Same difference. They used the same damn inflatable kiddie pool filled with sand every year and half the girls showed up in bikini tops until the school decided that went against dress code and finally changed the theme to stop it. Don't remember what it became. That was a couple years after I graduated and way before my boys went to the school."

Brittney let out a long sigh, which came across easily through the phone. "Good. You really are who you say you are. Only a longtime local would know that bit of trivia. And I'm speaking to Sheriff West? The new female sheriff that's turning everything on its head?"

So she did know who Rebecca was. Which meant referring to her as a man was a test to see if they got it wrong.

Why is she so unwilling to believe we're who we said?

Rebecca had been called paranoid before, but this woman was next level.

Hoyt rubbed his neck. "Not sure I would say that to her

face when she's the one writing the duty roster, but yes, ma'am, that was Sheriff Rebecca West who answered you earlier. I'm standing in your house, which is a crime scene, with the sheriff and Special Agent in Charge Benson, like he said."

"I'm sorry about all the questions, folks. But getting a phone call like this is pretty strange. I wanted to confirm your identities. Can't be too careful."

Benson's gray-streaked eyebrows crowded together in the middle of his forehead. "Well, if you'd like, I can send federal agents to come pick you up and bring you in, if that would help to convince you."

Brittney laughed. "Sorry, Benson, but you'd have to send the *Federales*. I'm somewhere south of the border. And you'll never get me back on that forsaken island. Ever." She seemed adamant. "Now that I know you are who you say you are, and I'm sure Sheriff West wouldn't let anyone impersonate a federal agent, I'll happily answer any questions you have. And maybe even a few you don't."

Everything about her voice implied she was calm and comfortable now.

What the fuck? Hoyt mouthed to Rebecca, but she shook her head. She had no idea either.

"Is your husband there with you?" Benson pressed forward with his questions, ignoring the pop quiz Brittney had issued.

"No, he's not. And I'm under the impression I won't be seeing him again."

"What gives you that impression?" Rebecca was almost scared to ask.

"Because I received his dick in the mail with a note apologizing for any inconvenience his untimely death might have caused. It was signed Francesco Amado."

Rebecca leaned away from the phone. Francesco Amado

was the head of the Amado cartel. It was the same cartel that had tried to establish territory around the island and failed.

She glanced around the well-appointed home. As she'd suspected, there was no way a Select Board member would be able to afford all this without some outside help.

"You'll forgive me if I sell my house and get the hell out of Dodge?"

"Why didn't you report this?"

"I keep up with friends there. I know what those cartel people did to you and your team, Sheriff. Do you think I'm going to stick my neck out? Arrest me if you can find me."

"We do have that power, Mrs. Longfellow. When was the last time you spoke to your husband?" Benson was smooth in his threat, but it didn't faze Brittney. Rebecca supposed that once you'd faced your husband's dismembered penis in a box, there wasn't much that could affect you.

"Please, call me Brittney. And the last time I spoke to him in person was in June. He's always very busy with his job in the summer, so we rarely got to spend any time together."

"What about on the phone? We need to establish a timeline."

"We stopped speaking mid-July? Early August? I can't remember."

"Does he have a phone number I can track?" Benson pulled a pen from his pocket, ready to write down a number.

Brittney gave it to him. "But I don't think it'll help you."

Rebecca couldn't restrain herself. "Don't you want to find your husband's killer?"

Brittney laughed. "Sheriff West, I'm pretty sure *you* have already taken care of his actual killer. Mitchell was involved in so much wheeling and dealing between the cartel and those Yacht Club people, I'm surprised he wasn't killed sooner. Not that I know any specifics. I learned not to ask questions if I don't want the answers. And I rarely want the answers."

There was something so bleak and hopeless in her words that Rebecca couldn't think of anything else to say. Benson explained to the woman that they'd be going through her home, hunting for evidence, and she gave them her full permission.

"Just make sure it's in saleable condition when you're done."

Benson scratched his jaw. "Mrs. Longfellow—"

"Brittney."

"I have to advise you to come to Shadow Island. You have potentially been involved in illegal activity—"

"Special Agent, if you find anything to connect me to my husband's dealings, by all means, come and find me. In the meantime, you don't have a pot to piss in, and I've been cooperative. So the next person you'll hear from, if you hear from me ever again, will be my attorney. Have a lovely day."

After the call ended, the sheriff, deputy, and special agent all looked at one another.

"Does this mean this house might be a murder site?" Hoyt asked.

"Forensics will be here soon. We can ask them once they've had a chance to evaluate the scene." Benson looked both annoyed and amused at Brittney Longfellow's attitude. "How much blood does a dismembered penis generate?"

Rebecca snorted. "I guess we'll find out."

20

Rebecca slowly spun around as she surveyed the foyer, taking in the area from the front door to the open floor space next to the stairs. She checked for any clues to where Longfellow might've gone. Could there be more hidden storage nooks like the one under the stairs? Maybe the intruder was after something Longfellow left behind.

"The last time anyone saw Mitchell Longfellow was August third. Which was right after he'd been contacted by Chester Able. Was he still caught up in drug running?"

Special Agent Benson looked at Rebecca sharply. "It sounds like I'm going to need to get caught up on things."

"You're not the only one," Rebecca grumbled as she tried to put together all the seemingly disconnected pieces.

They had two possible home intruders, one who'd been upstairs, one who'd been entering the back door. Based on the bank bags, Rebecca believed one of the intruders was their bank robber, and she imagined this empty house had looked like a good place to hole up.

Was it by mere chance that the bank robber had picked this house to stay in? Possibly. But there were no signs of a break-in. Did he know a way in? Was he familiar with the Longfellows?

And the man wearing the ski mask was a strange addition to the puzzle. Had he been here to rob Longfellow? Perhaps he was a cartel member come to retrieve things from the murdered man? Or was he just a burglar who was casing an expensive, abandoned house?

Two criminals in a third criminal's house isn't a coincidence.

"How much longer until your forensics techs get here?"

Benson checked his watch. "They should be here in about twenty."

"Then let's go ahead and do a quick walk-through. Deputy Frost, where did you say those bags were?"

Hoyt pointed up the stairs. "In the master bedroom. And it seems like the squatter, the bank robber, whatever you want to call him, went through the closet too. I can't tell if anything's missing, but if he left a bag here, he might've swapped it out for a new one he'd found."

"That would make sense." Rebecca turned to head up the stairs. Hoyt went first, leading them to the master bedroom.

Upstairs wasn't as dedicated to blatant luxury as downstairs. While everything still looked to be high end, there weren't the ostentatious displays of wealth. Considering the Longfellow who Rebecca knew, she was betting he flaunted his wealth in areas where guests were sure to see it.

Despite all the framed art pieces on the walls downstairs, there wasn't a single picture of his family. Not one of Mitchell and his parents, no wedding photos, graduation snapshots, nothing that displayed the people who were supposed to be living here.

It was a three-bedroom home, and all the doors had been left open from Hoyt and Viviane clearing the house while searching for the intruder. The room closest to the stairs was set up as a guest room. The next room had a very feminine feel to it but was a bedroom and office combo. Rebecca wondered if that was Brittney's room.

Her theory about Brittney and Mitchell having their own rooms seemed more plausible as she walked into the last and biggest bedroom. She stepped in and turned a slow circle. It was starkly masculine with a king-size mahogany sleigh bed. There were two matching bedside tables, one of which was empty. The other held an array of men's watches still in their boxes.

That was all the furniture in the room. Not a single dresser, vanity, or storage box occupied any of the plentiful floor space.

There was another door in the corner. When Rebecca went in to get a closer look, she found the en suite bathroom. The shower mat in front of the marble-tiled shower was damp, suggesting someone had used it recently.

A fluffy blue towel lay on the counter, and a smaller matching one was on the floor near the door. Both appeared damp. Towels, toothbrushes, and shampoo bottles would all need to be bagged. Faucets, shower door handles, and even the flush knob on the toilet would require fingerprinting. The sink, counter, and floor would also need to be thoroughly searched for stray hairs.

Considering how many clothes had been pulled out and dumped on the floor, those would need to be taken in and checked to find the squatter's original clothing, which might not even be in the pile. They'd also need to get a DNA sample from Longfellow to compare. Maybe if they were lucky, some of Mitchell's hair would be present in the brush resting on the bathroom counter.

Only men's clothing hung in the walk-in closet. Other articles of clothing had been shoved aside, leaving them dangling precariously from their hangers.

There was also a generic black t-shirt amid the pile, which did not match any of the other clothing in the closet. Mitchell seemed to be the type of guy who preferred all his clothing to be hung up. Even his boxers hung from clips on hangers.

Although there were many details Rebecca wanted to know about Mitchell Longfellow, the fact that he wore silk and bamboo cotton boxers was not on that list. Nor that he was finicky enough to hang them in a closet. Yet, there she was.

Most of the clothes were business suits, followed by a small mix of business casual garments, and very few items she'd call street clothes. In fact, there were only two pairs of jeans and no shorts as far as she could see. She couldn't imagine paying so much to live near the beach without owning a single pair of shorts to enjoy the sun.

"So what makes you think Mitchell ran?" Benson peered around the room as he pulled on his gloves. "It seems to me that most of his possessions are still here."

Hands on her knees, Rebecca knelt to take a mental inventory of the stacks of messenger bags and man purses, all made of high-quality leather, lined up in the bottom of the closet. "Well, to be honest, it was the state police who determined that Longfellow had most likely fled. At the time, I was recovering in the hospital from the cartel ambush. I trusted their reporting on the matter. That was a state police investigation, though, so you'll have to follow up with them."

That whole investigation was something she still didn't like to think about, especially how it ended…

She briefly thought about making another trip to D.C. to visit Darian's grave. He'd like to know that Longfellow had paid the price for his part in the hell they'd gone through.

Hey, Darian…Longfellow lost his long fellow. She could just imagine how the late deputy would have laughed at that.

There was a noticeable gap in the line of bags. "It was supposed to be a state police sting. We were merely acting as the lookout while the state police hung back with the Coast Guard, ready to swoop in as soon as the boat from the drug cartel showed up. Neither of those things happened. Instead, we were ambushed on the island shortly after making landfall and our ride was out of sight."

"Where was this?"

"It's called Little Quell Island." Hoyt lifted his gaze from the camera where he was taking pictures of the bedside table. "It's more of a spit of land than an actual island. Not big enough to sustain more than a few birds at a time. But it's got a lot of trees and sadly a lot of places to hide. Which is why we planned to get there before the cartel was set to make their drop."

"So it was the drug cartel men who ambushed you?"

She focused on the clothes, trying to figure out if any didn't belong. "We didn't know who ambushed us at the time, but after we got their bodies to the morgue, we ran their fingerprints. The guy in charge, Wesley Garrett, was a known runner for the Amado Cartel. He had a record of violent crimes and gun and drug running."

Rebecca pulled the digital camera from her pocket and started taking pictures of the clothes that had been strewn across the floor. "We know Garrett killed two drug dealers with likely associations with the Yacht Club. He also tried to kill a third."

"Like I said before," Benson shook his head, "you sure have had a lot of weird things going on down here."

"You know the funny part about this, though?" Rebecca continued taking pictures, focusing on the black shirt first. FBI forensics would be here soon to do the same thing, but she liked having her own photos to refer to.

"We only recently got done being investigated by the state

police for having such a high crime rate. Only to realize *they* were the ones that had dropped the ball on this. I mean, didn't they follow up on Mitchell at all?" She turned to Hoyt.

"I don't know what they did, Boss. Had a lot on my plate at the time and was more than willing to let Rhonda and her crew resolve all the issues. When they told me Mitchell skipped town, it made perfect sense to me. He wasn't a suspect or a person of interest, and him leaving like he did wasn't illegal. All we had were a few follow-up questions." Hoyt shrugged. "I screwed up. That's on me."

Rebecca looked over at him. His mouth was twisted, and the corners of his eyes drooped down, highlighting the crow's feet he'd developed from smiling so much. "It's not on your head, Frost. This was Rhonda's case and her oversight. There was no reason for us to investigate it."

Benson pulled a tablet out and began tapping on the screen. She couldn't tell if he was trying to make himself appear busy or was looking into something.

She returned her focus to her senior deputy. "We need to dig in here. If Longfellow was killed, I doubt they took him off the island to handle it. Garrett wouldn't have had that kind of time." She laughed harshly, and he glanced over, guilt still lingering in his eyes. "And now I get to give Rhonda a hard time for screwing up."

"Or I can." Benson spoke from the middle of the room. "You're talking about Special Agent Rhonda Lettinger with the General Investigation Section?"

Rebecca shifted her attention toward Benson, who was reading something on his tablet. Most likely the case file, if he knew Rhonda's name. "That's the one."

"Feel free to give her a good-natured hard time. If you do it soon enough, you might even be able to give her a warning that I'll be sending someone over to ask her some pointed questions."

Rebecca knew the hard light in his eyes. Standing, she pulled her phone from her pocket. There was an FBI building in Norfolk not too far from where Rhonda worked. Rebecca was willing to bet an agent was already on their way over.

"Hey, Boss. I think we've got some fingerprints."

Rebecca paused.

"There's a thick layer of dust here. You can see where someone touched the watches. And the table's coated in a high-gloss shellac too." Hoyt knelt, getting a better angle on the marks.

Viviane's voice crackled through the radio. "Sheriff, Frost, the FBI techs are here."

"Thanks, Darby. Tell them we're upstairs in the last bedroom at the end of the hall." Rebecca leaned over but couldn't see the marks Hoyt was talking about from where she was standing next to the closet. "They'll get a print for us, Frost."

"Do you have prints from Dillon Miller to compare them to?" Benson checked what Hoyt had found.

"You mean our local Dillon?"

Benson gave her a grim look. "I think we'd be looking for a local, wouldn't we? Someone who might know this house was unoccupied?"

He had a point.

"We don't have Dillon's prints. But we can always compare them later, once we catch him. I don't have hundreds of agents sitting at their desks ready to run data and track down people, Benson. The deputies with me are all I have. We still don't even know if it's Shadow Island Dillon Miller or another one of the many scattered around the region. It's a common name."

He didn't look convinced. "Maybe."

An idea sparked in Rebecca's mind. "What we do have is a

familial match for his DNA. His father is in prison, and we got a sample from him as part of that case. I'll go downstairs and make sure the plate and cup are collected. Hopefully, we can get a sample from that, then compare it to Owen Miller's."

Benson nodded and went back to typing. Hopefully, he was getting one of his agents to track down all the Dillon Millers like she'd hinted. She already had her people working long hours, as they had been all summer and fall. They needed a break before they all burned out.

Knowing she was running low on time to warn Rhonda, Rebecca jogged down the hall and bounded down the stairs. The techs were already setting up, taking pictures and placing evidence markers while Viviane watched them. She asked the techs to make sure to collect the plate and cup from the den before heading out the front door.

Rebecca found a quiet spot to make her call.

Thankfully, Rhonda was in the office, and Rebecca quickly filled her in on what was happening. Rhonda was not happy about the slack job her staff had done and appreciated the heads up.

Rebecca disconnected and walked back inside.

"Hey, Sheriff?"

She stopped a few inches inside the foyer and turned to the tech who had called out to her. It was a woman in her mid-forties kneeling on the floor in the den with a pair of magnifying glasses over her eyes, making her appear deranged and owllike.

"Yes?" Rebecca didn't know her name.

"Have you had a call out here before? For say, a murder? Or..." She trailed off as she chewed on a thought. "Or maybe a stabbing incident or something. In the last year or so?"

That was one hell of a way to get everyone's attention. Rebecca walked over, her heartbeat increasing. Maybe this was the murder scene after all. "No. What did you find?" The floor seemed perfectly normal to her.

"I've got bleach and scrub damage on this recliner. It blends in with the leather, but it's easy enough to spot on the stitching. Add to that, there's minute kerf marks on the hardwood floor here, as well as bleach damage under this polyurethane."

Though she pointed, Rebecca still saw nothing. "May I borrow your eyes, please?"

The tech grinned. "The poly is much fresher in these areas than the rest of this room. That means it was applied more recently than the surrounding pieces. It also tells me this was a professional cleaner who did the job. And I don't mean an accredited one. Someone wanted this scene to go unnoticed and put in the time and effort to hide all the evidence."

Well, of course they did.

"You're telling me that someone bled a lot in this room?" Checking around, Rebecca thought everything seemed perfectly normal. But to the tech's experienced eyes, there was a hidden story.

The woman nodded. "Here, here, here, here, and here." She pointed to five different spots on the floor.

Getting closer, Rebecca thought she might be able to make out slightly paler and shinier lines on the floor.

"From the layout and sizes, plus the blood I'm seeing sprayed around, I'd say someone was cut up here. Maybe with a power saw. It'd be really hard to do without power tools." The tech pointed to the foyer and kitchen. "This is a much smarter place to do it than on those tile floors. They'd chip and break. Makes it a lot harder to hide where the saw nicked the floors."

"Well, damn." Rebecca had been so intent trying to see the tiny details she hadn't noticed Benson walk up behind her. "It seems more and more likely Longfellow died right here. We might have to check the yard for him, or for pieces of him."

Rebecca thought back to the murder of Abe Barclay. The caretaker of the local cemetery had been alive when Mitchell went missing. "Actually, you might want to bring in ground-penetrating radar and check the cemetery too. There might be more bodies buried there than on record. We had a cemetery caretaker who was working with a known assassin. God only knows what they did out there, and I don't have enough sway to get cleared to do the job myself."

"Seriously, Rebecca. What the hell is going on in your little town?" Benson and several of his people were staring at her.

The weight of the question settled on Rebecca's shoulders like an elephant.

"More than even I thought, according to your tech here."

21

Keeping my head down, I tried to stop my hands from shaking as I walked out of the small convenience store. I unboxed my new burner phone and went through the quick setup routine.

It was a bit shocking that a town this small would have so many places that sold burners. The dude behind the counter hadn't batted an eye when I'd paid cash.

This island was full of high-class criminals needing untraceable phones, I supposed.

The phone finally chimed, letting me know it was finished booting up. I'd memorized the number I needed to call, a requirement of this job. I opened the texting app and shot off a quick message, telling Albert his safe house had been compromised but not to worry, I'd gotten away clean.

Maybe not as clean as he'd like, but I could ponder that later.

The whole situation was fucked up.

All I cared about was that I hadn't been caught. I'd barely had the time to grab my money before cutting and running.

I'd had to hold my breath against the after-stink of the pepper spray that woman had used.

Who the hell was she?

And who the hell was the guy downstairs?

Whoever it was had been long gone by the time I hit the backyard, shifting through the junipers back the way I'd come. After grabbing my things from the master bedroom, I hadn't stuck around. Hopefully, there was nothing left behind to incriminate me. Part of the job was to always prepare for the worst. That was why I'd already packed my clothes and the cash in my go bag.

This island was crawling with bad people. Or maybe there was something to the old witch curse stories. It was a miracle the safe house, so full of treasures, hadn't been robbed earlier.

Maybe the woman was a maid they forgot to cancel, or a ride they didn't remember to tell me about, or just a nosy neighbor. It didn't matter. Without a message from Albert telling me to expect someone, anyone who approached me was a threat.

I knew Albert would be slow to respond.

Just because I was young didn't mean I was stupid. I wasn't carrying any identification and hadn't been since I got the rental car. That license, with the false information I needed to rent the car, had been given to me by Albert at a dead drop.

Apparently, I was a dead ringer for the guy whose identity I'd borrowed. As soon as I was done using the ID, I'd tossed it into the garbage. It was an adequate forgery but wouldn't stand up to police scrutiny. Hell, I wouldn't even have trusted it against an experienced bartender.

I had no idea what I was supposed to be doing right now, so I made it up as I went along.

Adjusting the black backpack, I headed away from the convenience store toward the place I would blend in the best.

The beach, where everyone on the coast went if they weren't tied to a desk. The location wasn't ideal, but I could still make it work. Not having a swimsuit, I had to improvise. It helped that today was a chilly day, and the middle of the week, so there weren't a lot of people around.

Holding the phone in front of my face, I acted like I was taking video as I walked down the public access to the beach.

Monologuing as I strolled, like I was doing a live video, helped my disguise.

Teens would give me a wide berth because they'd respect what they thought I was doing. Older people would turn away in disgust because they either didn't know what the hell I was doing or because they despised vloggers and influencers.

It was hard to believe I was better at this crap than the guy who'd hired me. Then again, I supposed that was *why* he had hired me. I could do the shit he couldn't. Still, it'd be nice if Albert would at least act like what I was doing was important. Fifteen minutes, and he still hadn't responded.

Moving to the edge of the water, I sent another message. I reminded good ole Al that the longer I was out and about in public, the more likely I was to be seen, remembered, or picked up by the cops. I added that neither of us wanted that.

He had as much to lose as I did if I got caught. Maybe more.

On the beach, I avoided security cameras, but that didn't mean I was totally safe. As one of the only people out here, I was in a quandary. Stay here and not run into people? Or move to a more populated area where I could blend in? Farther up the beach, I saw a pier. It wasn't packed, but at least I'd be less conspicuous up there.

Keeping my face turned toward the ocean, I headed that

way. With every pace, I hoped for word from Albert. Some indication of what the next steps should be.

We were on a tight timeline. If they wanted me to upload the virus, I needed access to the bank accounts. But without the safe house, I was high and dry. Since Plan A hadn't panned out and Plan B had been compromised by randoms walking into the safe house, he needed to let me know what Plan C was.

I made it to the end of the pier. Still nothing.

Maybe he wasn't going to respond. Could he be ignoring me? Leaving me to twist in the wind? My heart rate sped up thinking about that. Leaving town would be a lot harder on my own.

I could toss the gun, toss the phone, and take the money south of the border. Once I hit Mexico, they'd be more than happy to exchange my American *dólares* for *pesos*. Then I'd be invisible.

Watching the water shift and spin the slimy jellyfish caught in the waves, a pang of jealousy hit me.

Maybe I could toss myself in the ocean. Not come out until I reached Mexico.

The thought did have a certain appeal.

A tinny chime sounded, and it took me a moment to realize it was the notification sound on my new phone. Finally.

Albert had nothing to say about the safe house or its unscheduled guest. But he did say there was a motel in town. I could get a room there if I spoke to the owner and said I was working for him. That was absolute bullshit and totally unacceptable, and I told him that.

Another day here? What the actual fuck?

He replied quickly this time.

You've still got a job to do. You don't want to leave it incomplete.

He had me over a barrel. They had damning evidence against me.

Worse, they were clearly willing to eliminate anyone who didn't do as they *asked*.

I thought of the head in a box somewhere in the ocean.

There was no doubt in my mind that if I disobeyed, they'd throw me to the wolves. At the very least they might sic their pet cop on me and add resisting arrest charges to whatever kind of beating I'd be given prior to getting booked. Double-crossing them wasn't an option.

I jammed the phone in my pocket and started walking back toward town, leaving my daydreams of swimming to freedom to rot on the pier like a gutted fish.

22

Rebecca drove Benson into downtown Shadow Island, pulling into the law enforcement parking spot in front of town hall. According to the report Rhonda filed, Richmond Vale was the one who claimed Mitchell Longfellow had left town for other business opportunities. Vale's word, as Longfellow's boss, convinced the state police that he'd left Shadow Island after not being seen for a week.

Even Benson agreed that the state police hadn't messed up. They'd spoken to Longfellow's wife and boss to verify his whereabouts. There was no reason to suspect anything.

Now there was an APB out until they could confirm his death. His wife might have seen his penis—if it was indeed his penis—but that wasn't necessarily a mortal wound, though it didn't bode well...

But the FBI wasn't as easy to fool as the state police were. And Benson didn't merely want answers—he wanted proof. That was why they headed down to the offices of the Select Board. This was also official Shadow Island business, since it was the treasurer who went missing.

The purpose of the trip was not for Rebecca to turn the

tables on Richmond Vale by yelling at him in his own office. She'd leave that to Benson.

As she got out of her SUV, she casually reached up and pressed the record button on her pen. This was something she knew everyone in the sheriff's office would enjoy watching later.

Benson led the way, his long, heavy strides sounding like slow thunder in the empty halls as he followed the signs to the offices of the mayor and Select Board members. The receptionist for those offices, a rail-thin woman with bottle-blond hair and professionally short nails, stared at them, first as Benson stormed up to her desk, then while Rebecca went through the formality of presenting her badge.

"Ms. Pendleton, Sheriff Rebecca West to see Select Board Chairman Richmond Vale on an urgent matter."

The receptionist, Marcy Pendleton, timidly bobbed her head as she picked up the phone. "Mr. Vale, the sheriff is here to see you." She pressed her hand against the receiver of the phone. "He says he doesn't want to see you. He's on a very important phone call."

"I. Don't. Care." Rebecca spoke each word slowly and emphatically. "He needs to make himself available. This is an official inquiry. If he'd like, I can walk in there and take him down to the station to have a chat instead."

Pendleton bobbed her head again and repeated Rebecca's words. She flinched, dropping her eyes. "But, sir. Yes, I'll tell her exactly what you said." This time, she didn't cover the mouthpiece. She faced Rebecca directly, taking a moment to compose herself. "Mr. Vale insists that he doesn't have time for a 'shitty sheriff who can't do her job.'"

Benson squared his shoulders and dropped the full weight of his disapproving gaze on the receptionist. "How about for a damn fine FBI Special Agent in Charge on a case regarding a bank robbery, attempted murder, and a missing person?"

"Oh! Who's missing?" Pendleton seemed to forget Vale was still on the phone as she looked back and forth between Rebecca and Benson, her expression worried.

"As far as we can tell, Select Board Treasurer Mitchell Longfellow. Considering Richmond Vale was the only person who claims to have spoken to Longfellow in person since he went missing, he really needs to answer some questions." Benson leaned forward, looming over her even as he rested his hands on the edge of her desk. "When was the last time *you* saw him?"

"Him?" Pendleton squeaked. "You mean Mr. Longfellow? Not for the last month. At least. I filed his resignation paperwork back in August, I think. Are you saying he didn't move to take a better job?" She appeared genuinely confused.

"As far as we can tell, he never left the island. Which makes us wonder why your boss would tell us he did." Rebecca stretched her lips over her teeth, thoroughly enjoying this. If Pendleton didn't already know what a shitty piece of filth her boss was, she was about to find out. "How did you get that resignation letter? Did Vale give it to you? Or did Longfellow? Did he ever call after that? Or leave a forwarding address?"

"No." The receptionist shook her head. "He just stopped coming in one day. A couple of days later, I had his letter on my desk, and Mr. Vale said to file it, that Mr. Longfellow had quit and moved away." She jumped as Vale started yelling through the phone. "Yes, sir. I will. Yes, sir."

Hands shaking, she set the phone down. "He said you can go back." Turning, she pointed to the door in the middle of the room, almost directly behind her desk.

"Thank you, Marcy." Rebecca gave her a real smile before

walking around the receptionist's desk and pushing open the door to Richmond Vale's office.

It was small and cramped, with a large metal desk in the middle of the room, pressed against a wall on the right-hand side. There wasn't enough room for even a single bookcase. Even the desk was so small it barely accommodated the desktop and keyboard. The only personal touches appeared to be two picture frames, though she couldn't see the details of the photos.

Rebecca surmised this was the reason Dick hadn't wanted her to come back to his office. It was half the size of hers. She smirked down at him in his plastic chair.

Vale glowered up at her but didn't make any move to rise and greet her. "What do you want? What's this about the FBI having questions?"

Rebecca slid aside, gesturing as Benson stepped forward. "Special Agent in Charge Benson, this is Richmond Vale. The man who claims Mitchell Longfellow contacted him about resigning and moving away." It didn't need to be said again, but it was fun to watch Dick wriggle in discomfort.

"What right does the FBI have to come down here for something like this?" He spluttered, as if he was unsure of who to glare at.

"Something like what?" Benson didn't bother taking a chair. Instead, he stood straight, crossing his arms and scowling down at Vale. "What do you think 'this' is, Mr. Vale?"

"You said it was something to do with bank robbery, attempted murder, and a missing person. And I…you keep bringing up Mitchell. What's a bank robbery got to do with Mitchell?"

"We're not sure yet. However, it does involve Mr. Longfellow's residence. Every time we ask anyone about him, they all say the same thing. They haven't seen or spoken to the man since August third."

Rebecca bit back a smile. Benson was setting Vale up beautifully.

"Everyone except you," Benson continued. "When was the last time you saw your former colleague?"

"Sometime around then." He poked at his keyboard. "I got text messages and emails from him saying he was resigning. I believe he said it was because he was moving. I had no reason to think otherwise. Who else would email me from his account?"

"Anyone who had the proper login information. Did you even get a signature on his resignation letter?" Benson's face didn't give away much, but she knew he was fed up.

Rebecca stood silently, enjoying the show as Benson's stony expression brought sweat out on Vale's forehead.

"I'm not sure. You'd have to ask Marcy, my receptionist. She's the one who got the letter." He waffled his hand toward the door.

"We already did. She said it was sitting on her desk one morning, and you told her to go ahead and file it. Do you remember what day that was?" Rebecca bared her teeth. "If not, we can always go through your CCTV to check through that week until we find the person responsible for putting that letter on her desk."

"Don't you threaten me, West." Vale snarled and made as if he were going to stand up, then seemingly remembered Benson and stopped, staring at him.

"A threat?" Rebecca batted her eyelashes innocently. "I thought I was helping you. It seems someone was able to slip into your office and leave a letter of resignation on Marcy's desk. No one's questioning why a member of the Select Board suddenly disappeared. Don't you want to know what happened to Mitchell? I thought you two were friends."

He sneered at her. "Call it whatever you want. I doubt you'll be in office long enough to even get that warrant, let alone find anything untoward. I received an email from Mitchell saying he was resigning. The next day, his resignation letter was signed and on Marcy's desk. There's nothing suspicious about that. Even the state police agreed. And they did so in a timely manner and didn't need to hide behind their friends from the FBI."

"I'd like to see that resignation letter." Benson's voice was a low growl as he took the last possible step forward, his legs pressing against the front of Vale's desk. "And I'm not here as a friend. I'm here to solve a federal crime. If you get in my way, if you slow me down, I will haul you in for obstructing a federal investigation." He smiled, and it was easily as toothy and feral as Rebecca's had been. "In case you're wondering, *that* was a threat."

"Do whatever you want." Vale tried to lean back in his chair casually, but his hand trembled as he waved them both off. He was a slippery one. "I've done nothing wrong. And I'm sure once we get a competent sheriff to take over the office, things will calm down again."

Rebecca rolled her eyes. The weasel had been threatening to take her job away since the first time she'd met him. The man was all bark and no bite. And he had no real power to remove her from the position.

"Yes. Things will be much better once Sheriff Burke takes that badge off your chest."

Burke!

"The state trooper who was so bad at maintaining a crime scene, he got chewed out by the agent in charge and sent back to his sergeant to get disciplined?" Rebecca laughed. "He was so bad, his *sergeant* got chewed out too."

Seemingly pissed at having his threat fall flat, Dick jerked upright again.

Rebecca didn't give him a chance to say anything else. "If he's the man you think is best for the job, make sure you vote for him. But don't forget. I'm not the only one who's up for election this November. The entire Select Board is as well. And you haven't exactly been making friends these last six months. We're going to get answers as to why Longfellow's chair is empty and who made it that way."

"You—"

"We'll just go ask Marcy for that resignation letter." Rebecca turned for the door. "According to the Virginia Freedom of Information Act, that will be public record. So will the CCTV footage. We don't need a warrant for those."

23
___

Rebecca parked the SUV in front of Longfellow's house once more. The ride back from town hall had been quiet. She and Benson watched a man in full personal protective equipment walk out the front door carrying a plastic-wrapped chunk of hardwood flooring.

"This case keeps getting more complicated." Benson shot her an annoyed scowl as they walked up to the front door.

Despite what Rebecca had said as she left Dick's office, they weren't able to get a copy of Longfellow's resignation letter or even see it to check his signature. It was too late in the day and Marcy had conveniently left. And then Vale insisted that the office could take a "reasonable amount of time" to locate the paper. In the end, they'd gotten in the cruiser empty-handed to head back to the crime scene.

Neither she nor Benson were happy about that, but there was nothing they could do after business hours. Fortunately, the clock was ticking. If the town didn't produce that letter, she had no doubt Benson would follow through on his threat and arrest Dick for obstruction.

She could freely admit to herself that she hoped Vale

didn't produce the letter. They could always retrieve it after he'd been hauled off to jail.

They stopped in the foyer. A large sheet of plastic tarp had been spread over the hardwood, and teams of technicians were working to wrap up more bundles of wood flooring.

"Boss." Hoyt waved from where he was standing on the stairs, leaning against the railing.

She and Benson walked over, keeping out of the way of the hardworking FBI personnel.

"They found a pool of blood under the floorboards. Every time they pull up one slat, there's more under it. They've been going at this for the whole time you've been gone. The puddle goes under the boards in every direction. It's not looking good for Longfellow."

Benson turned to the doorway that led into the den. "Do they think it's from more than one body?"

"Not as far as I've heard. But they keep working their way out from the main blood pool. Best I could tell, before I had to move back here to get out of the way, it could end up being a full body's worth of blood." Hoyt shrugged as if it didn't matter. And maybe it didn't. His stomach was notoriously weak.

So far, there was nothing more gruesome than some wooden slats with bloodstains on the back of them.

"Could be one person or several. That's why they want to get all the wood, to test each one and see how many donors are in it."

"How far have they gotten?" Personally intrigued, Rebecca tried to see if there was some way of moving closer to sneak a peek at the mess.

"So far, both recliners have been taken out. And boxes of stuff from the lower couple rows of shelves. I'd guess about forty square feet of flooring too. Blood had soaked into the concrete slab, and they're still searching for the edge of the pool." He jerked his head upward, indicating the second floor. "Everything from the master bedroom has come out, including the top layer of the bed itself. Hell, they even took the P-traps from the sinks in both bathrooms and the kitchen."

"I'm glad they're being thorough." Hearing more commotion upstairs, Rebecca turned. Two men in navy blue windbreakers tromped down the stairs carrying boxes. She peeked inside as they passed and saw Longfellow's clothing along with what appeared to be the contents of his entire medicine cabinet.

"Deborah has her work cut out for her." Rebecca leaned against the banister. "This place is a disaster area and the probable site of a murder. Bad news for Brittney. She's not going to get her asking price."

"Probably the least of her worries." Benson also inspected the boxes as they went past.

"Frost, this is going to go on all night. Head back to the station. Darby can go too. You two still need to write up your reports." Rebecca glanced at her watch. "Actually, scratch that. Just go on home. There's no need to get those done tonight. We're already basically caught up, and we'll check with the techs if we have questions. You've done more than enough for the day."

"You don't need to tell me twice, Boss. Benson." Hoyt tipped his hat to the special agent. "I promised myself a vanilla shake at Betty's if we got out of here early enough."

Rebecca watched him go, then turned her attention back to the blue-clad workers disassembling and hauling off various pieces of the house. "How many crimes do you think we're going to uncover with all this?"

Benson grunted. "I'm only concerned about the one. Of course, I'm more than happy to give you information about any others we uncover as we go. Did you see how deeply that blood was soaked through the untreated bottoms of the wood?"

"All the way, as far as I could tell. The first tech said there were kerf marks under the varnish too."

"Which means that incident is older than the bank robbery." Benson's gaze slid around while betraying no hint of what he was thinking.

"Around August third might be a good bet. There's been enough time for the cleanup to happen and for the bleach and varnish smells to dissipate." Rebecca stood silent for a moment. "But what would've caused Dillon Miller to do this? It doesn't quite track for me. What would trigger it? Losing two people so close to him? Guilt over Wallace's death? Even if he snapped, going after Longfellow doesn't make sense."

"I couldn't tell you what makes people do violent things." Benson's shoulders seemed to slump under the weight of the world.

Rebecca pointed at various expensive items around the house that hadn't been hauled away by forensics. "Why would Dillon risk robbing a bank when he already had access to everything stored here? That collection of watches on the nightstand was most likely worth more than he collected from the tellers."

"True. However, some of the items are so rare that pawning them might alert the authorities."

She snorted. "You mean like robbing a bank?"

Benson turned to face her, frowning. "I think that's our central question. What does our perpetrator, whoever he is, have to gain? And how does this tie to the bank robbery? Or *does* it? The whole situation is so strange."

Two more techs came down the stairs carrying boxes. Benson stopped the first tech and reached into a bag perched on top of the pile inside.

He pulled out a cheap mobile phone. Keeping it in the bag, Benson pressed the center key and the screen lit up.

It was shocking. Most people in a situation like this would make sure they'd set a screen lock of some kind. Benson scowled at the phone, then turned it so Rebecca could see.

The text messaging app was open. And one of the last texts it received was the address of Longfellow's house.

She grunted when she noticed that the only messages on the phone were about the house, including directions on how to enter without being seen. Text messages were easy to erase, but forensic techs could often recover deleted messages.

"More questions and no answers. Who sent the robber to this address? If it was Dillon who committed the robbery, why would he need Longfellow's address at all? He's a local."

Benson scrolled down and whistled. "Well, I think it's even more interesting…"

"What?" Rebecca took the phone from him and read the very final texts.

Are you sure no one lives here?

Yes.

How do you know?

Because the owner's head is currently in a box at the bottom of the ocean.

24

The sun was already well above the horizon when Rebecca parked her truck at the sheriff's station the next morning. As she hopped out, she got an odd sense of being tardy. For the last few days—or had it been weeks?—she'd been coming in early.

Cases spilled from one day to the next, making it hard to remember. Either way, it had been going on for so long that coming in on time now felt late.

But for just a moment, she had a tiny window of peace and tranquility. Closing her eyes, she lifted her face to the sun and simply basked in it. As she leaned back against her driver's door, warmth radiated into her muscles, forcing her to recognize how tense they were. Lifting her travel mug to her lips, she sipped her coffee and rotated her shoulders, telling her muscles to relax and enjoy the day.

This was what she used to do at home after leaving work. Now she was doing it at work after leaving home. Living with someone else was so much more stressful than she'd imagined.

Just a few more weeks. Then things can get back to normal.

An approaching car engine made her open her eyes.

Jake's slate-gray Jeep Wrangler pulled into the lot, and her moment of placid solitude ended as he leaned out his window to talk to her.

"You all right there, Boss?"

"Simply enjoying the sun and my coffee before going in." Rebecca raised her mug to him.

He gave a nod and parked on the other side of her truck.

She pushed off the sun-warmed metal of her door and joined him to walk inside. "How are you settling into life here on Shadow Island?"

"I haven't, really. I'm still under lease at my apartment in Coastal Ridge. Work's good, though. You've got a good group of people here. Have you heard anything about that bank manager yet?"

It was the most words Rebecca had heard Jake string together since she'd interviewed him for the position of deputy. And he'd neatly guided the topic back to work and the case they were working on. She'd noticed that about him from the beginning, that he liked to keep his private life to himself. And she respected that.

"The doctors managed to stabilize him. Not out of the woods yet, though, and never awake for long enough to do more than squeeze his mother's hand. She's been at his bedside this whole time, since she was able to get a ride down."

Jake reached the door first and held it open for her. "He's going to make a full recovery, then?"

Rebecca shook her head. "They say that's still to be determined. The doctors aren't giving us a lot of information."

"Because of HIPAA. Of course." Jake stepped in behind her and gave a nod of greeting to Elliot, who was leaning forward on the desk, smiling broadly.

"I know Benson's calling the hospital for updates every few hours, and most likely pissing off the staff. That's why I'm only calling once every morning. Otherwise, they've said they'll call if anything significant changes." Rebecca leaned into the half door so the fob on her keychain would unlock it. "And the only real suspect we have is a man of basic height and build who might or might not be named Dillon Miller. We need to track down more leads on this case, and I'm getting tired of waiting for Benson's group to do that."

Elliot was still stretched forward, hanging on their every word.

Jake cocked his head at the young man. "Did you need something, Elliot?"

"Something to do might be nice." The dispatcher perked up. "I never realized how lonely and boring this job could be. It's so quiet."

Jake laughed and nudged Rebecca, who was already shaking her head. He placed a hand over his mouth to hide his smirk before warning Elliot. "Enjoy days like this, young grasshopper. For they are few and far between."

Rebecca tried to appear stern. "Relish them and the peaceful silence they bring. Never take them for granted. And never say the dreaded Q word."

Elliot frowned, one eye squinting. "Oh, you mean because it's so quiet? Why?"

Rebecca and Jake both groaned and stopped in their tracks.

Elliot sat up straight, startled.

"I told you not to say that." Rebecca pointed an accusing finger at the dispatcher. "When things blow up today, remember it's all on you. And don't come crying when a situation gets completely out of hand. You're the one who jinxed us."

"For at least a week." Jake shook his head sadly.

Rebecca gestured dramatically at Elliot as she walked back to the coffee station, though she had a hard time keeping a smile off her face. "Why does every rookie have to do that?"

"No clue." Jake shook his head again and settled in at his desk. "I remember the first time I screwed up like that. We ended up with a twenty-car pileup on the interstate. With smaller cascading wrecks happening for the rest of the day from rubberneckers."

"Mine was a flood of bomb threats, called in to a bunch of newspapers and TV stations." Rebecca sighed, making sure Elliot could hear her.

"Sheriff?"

Rebecca finished pouring her coffee and turned around.

Elliot was leaning over the back of his seat, watching her. "Sheriff West, you were joking about that. Right?" He was starting to twist his headset cord nervously.

She couldn't hold back the smile that pulled at her lips, so she leaned into it and smiled wide. "Not at all. You can google it if you want. The Bureau ran me ragged, doing all the legwork that day after uttering the Q word."

Jake grunted loudly enough to make his entire body rock. "My sarge made me walk to each of the wrecks. Yeah, it was only over a three-mile area, but it was a lot of cars. That was the first pair of shoes I melted on the job."

"You melted your shoes?" Elliot spoke in a horrified whisper.

"Pavement gets hot on the interstates, especially in the middle of July." Jake sighed and lowered his head to work. "Boss, I'm going to check out Dillon's social media again. Maybe he's posted something new that'll help us. The agents trying to find him said he isn't registered as a student, and they can't find any rentals or campus housing under his name. They're checking to see if he's subletting a place, but so far, they've come up empty. They also haven't gotten back with the copy of the license used to rent the car."

Rebecca was impressed at how quickly Jake was able to immerse himself in his work. With all his skills, his lateral move to a small-town sheriff's station struck her as curious. She could ask Rhonda, but she'd rather wait for Jake to tell her. She trusted that he wasn't a mole sent to spy on them. But until Jake explained it when he was ready, the question of why he transferred would stay a mystery.

"Sounds good, Coffey. I'll ask Benson for an update on Dillon. Once you're done with that, start checking into the other Dillon Millers in the area. It's a very common name." Rebecca winked at Elliot before heading to her office.

Out of the corner of her eye, she could see the smirk on Jake's face before he covered it with his hand, pretending to be engrossed in his work.

"After I talk to Benson, I'm going to delve into Longfellow and check in with forensics. I know they're more thorough than our usual guys, but they seem to be taking an awfully long time to get back to us with any results."

Sitting down at her desk, she thought maybe today wouldn't be so bad after all. The first thing she did was file an official request for Longfellow's resignation letter along with any CCTV footage of him on the day he resigned. She needed to get eyes on whoever might be involved in covering up Longfellow's probable demise.

Knowing Vale was going to make this as difficult as possible, she made sure to email the request to him, the receptionist, the security company for the town hall, the mayor, and the Select Board members. Benson had most likely done the same thing the night before, but it was always fun to annoy Dick when she could. Hopefully, the elections would eliminate the need to work with him ever again.

She'd been so focused on her own election that she hadn't

looked to see who might be running against him. Which had been how he'd been able to surprise her with the name of her opponent, Burke. But there weren't any signs for Burke around town, and she briefly wondered if he was bluffing.

The local Office of Elections website had the information she wanted. Dolph Burke had filed his candidacy for sheriff. That was the bad news.

The good news made her clap with excitement. Meg Darby was running for Select Board chair.

That would be a real game changer. To have someone on the Select Board who wasn't actively hostile toward law enforcement and was also competent and friendly.

Better days might be just around the corner.

The FBI team was still going through Longfellow's house and all the records they could pull on him. The getaway car was still in the forensic shop, getting a thorough screening. She decided she wanted to circle back to something they'd learned previously but hadn't really had a chance to dig into.

Pulling up the BOLO they'd issued for the rental car used in the bank robbery, she found the report that was filed on the day it was towed. She was curious about the timing of the citation. It had gotten a ticket a few minutes after noon and was towed at three.

As Benson had said, the car had been parked in a grocery store parking lot on the island in one of the time-limited parking spaces. However, it was the one farthest from the front doors. A quick search showed that Benson's team had followed through already and learned there were no cameras in the parking lot or nearby businesses that covered that area.

Sure, he could have left his own car somewhere in the lot, rented the car, and then driven back to return his rental and retrieve his own car. But they'd searched the area around Longfellow's house for Dillon's dad's truck and didn't find it.

There'd been no reports of vehicles in that neighborhood left parked on the road overnight. And on that street where everyone had driveways and garages, a vehicle parked on the street would have stood out.

While they still had nothing concrete connecting their Dillon Miller to any of this, she wanted to clear him as a suspect as soon as possible.

Rebecca pulled up a map of the region, where she found the grocery store on Shadow Island deep within town. When she typed in the address of the rental agency in Coastal Ridge, she found it was clear on the north side of the city. The two locations were roughly eight miles away from each other.

How did he get back and forth? Even if he left his own car at the store before getting the rental, he still had to make it to the rental agency. A bus?

Finding the bus routes was easy enough. All the stops were clearly marked. One of them was just outside the shopping center for the grocery store. She jotted down the numbers for the buses that made stops there between nine a.m. and noon. Before closing the map, she noticed one long dotted line showing a route that left the city.

Scrolling out, she saw that it crossed the bridge leading to Coastal Ridge. The route only ran three times a day, so she rarely thought about it even being an option. Eight in the morning, four in the evening, eight at night.

That explained how he was able to get around without needing a car. Rebecca jotted down the number for the bus station and reached for her phone.

It rang before she could pick it up. "Sheriff Rebecca West, how can I help you?"

"Heya, Boss, it's me. I was talking to Elliot. You guys really freaked him out, but don't worry, I made it a lot worse."

Viviane's laughter made Rebecca smile. She knew she could count on Viviane to get in on the hazing.

"Which reminded me that I never followed through on that warrant last night. It should've come in, but we went out for shakes after you sent us home, so I couldn't check the fax."

Rebecca frowned. "Warrant for what?"

"The rental contract for the getaway car. They were being jerks and kept saying they weren't sure if they could hand it over, so I decided to stop playing nice and went ahead and requested a warrant for it. It's totally my screwup. I can come in and take care of that."

"No. Don't worry about it, Vi. I'll check the fax, and if it's there, I'll send Jake over to serve it."

"You sure, Boss?"

"Yeah, no worries. Enjoy your day off."

Rebecca went to the bullpen to check the fax machine.

As Viviane had anticipated, there was a signed warrant waiting for them. It had come in too late to be served last night. The rental agency wasn't a twenty-four-hour shop, so they hadn't even lost any time with Viviane's mistake. "Hey, Jake, can you go serve this warrant? It came through yesterday, but we got caught up with things at the secondary crime scene."

"Sure thing, Boss." Jake pushed away from his computer. "But you should check out Dillon's Instagram. You know him better than I do. I've never met the kid. Maybe you can make some sense of it."

"I'll check it out." Rebecca handed Jake the warrant and went to pull up what he'd found. She already had Dillon's Instagram handle memorized.

The post was a cartoon picture of a pair of eyes and ten words. *Keep an eye out here. I'm expecting some big news!*

"So you want someone to keep an eye on your Instagram

feed. But *why?*" The computer screen offered her no answers. His post didn't have a location. "Where are you, Dillon? And what's your big news? Do those cartoon eyes have some significance? Wherever you are, I hope you're safe and not doing something stupid."

As Rebecca turned on notifications for Dillon's feed, she wondered if his big news was going to be that he'd recently come into a lot of money. Young and cocksure criminals had posted about their criminal exploits before. Still, she wasn't sold on the idea that Dillon had turned so quickly to a life of crime. It would break her heart if she ended up having to arrest him.

25

The instant coffee the motel supplied was hardly more than sludge, but I managed to choke it down with enough of the powdered creamer and sugar. I'd slept like hell last night. The bed had been lumpy, the pillows flat, and the talk I'd heard in town kept repeating in my head.

They were talking about how the local real estate agent had come face-to-face with a masked man with a gun in one of the houses she had for sale. And now the house was swarming with the FBI. The Feds in such a small town was enough to get everyone's lips flapping.

No longer sure if I could trust Albert Gilroy, I found myself pondering everything Albert had ever said and reviewing this stupid plan he'd concocted.

Everything that had happened over the last day made less sense the more I thought about it. Why had a masked man with a gun broken into the Yacht Club's safe house while I was there? The real estate agent was explained, but the armed stranger wasn't.

Maybe the Yacht Club was done with me, trying to

eliminate me. That didn't make sense. I was doing everything they asked. I was following directions.

But I didn't get the transfer done. I didn't upload their virus.

Still, it wasn't the end of the world. We were trying again, weren't we?

Weren't we?

Surely, they didn't kill people over such trivial issues.

This was my first time working with Albert and his people. They had no reason to screw me over.

Were they mad I hadn't convinced Arthur Carson to work for them? They knew it was a possibility he'd refuse. I'd even been told what to do in case he didn't agree.

"Kill him and upload the virus."

Needing more noise around me, I'd turned on the TV when I woke up. A local station was airing the morning news. Weather, sports, traffic. Rinse and repeat. But my blood ran cold when they mentioned the bank robbery.

"Sources state that Arthur Carson, manager of the Sandpiper Bank, is expected to recover. The shooter has yet to be identified…"

Shit.

Arthur Carson hadn't died. Somehow, he'd survived an ass-whooping and a bullet to the chest. The news anchor praised the sheriff for acting so fast and credited her and her deputies for keeping him stable until paramedics arrived. Apparently, the old dude's mother was still around, and she was eternally grateful too.

Shit! This might be why Albert's been jerking me around. Because I failed to kill Carson. How was I supposed to know that shooting him in the chest wouldn't kill him?

I ran a hand through my hair, still weirded out by how short it was now. I'd picked up a box of bleach and a pair of scissors on my way to the motel last night. Looking in the mirror over the sink at the end of the room next to the bathroom door, I stared at myself.

My now orangey-blond short hair contrasted with a patchy but decent beard and mustache that I'd grown over the last couple of days. The old me was history. I'd grabbed a couple of suits from the safe house on a whim, so now I could pull off the young, trendy start-up businessman facade if I wanted.

As the news anchor switched back to the weather, my burner phone chimed.

Go to the boardwalk.

I debated responding, *Go to Hell*. Or ignoring it. I could still run. Not by doing something silly like jumping in the ocean, but simply by getting on a bus. I could head back to Coastal Ridge. From there, I could go to my place, get the rest of my stuff, and hit the road. I had my own car.

According to the news, they still didn't have any solid suspects for the robbery. The reports didn't mention me.

No one except the Yacht Club knew my identity. I could run. Hell, I could turn myself in to the cops, even. Say I was the squatter, but I had nothing to do with the bank or scaring that lady back at the house. That would…

Do nothing.

Shit.

The Yacht Club's cop, that statie who'd contacted me about working with Albert in the first place, had forced me into taking this job. Didn't really give me a choice. He'd knocked on my door to present me with a gift—a picture of me in a car, pulling off the gorilla mask I'd used on my last job.

His instructions from the Yacht Club had been to keep the evidence out of my criminal file…if I agreed to do a job for them. When I asked him why, he said they needed my services. If I cooperated, I could get a big payday. If not, I'd be looking at jail time.

Apparently, he could plant evidence or make it disappear. My choice.

If I went to the authorities, who would I see—the woman in charge or the cop who convinced me to take the job? He might shoot me on the spot, or I could have "an accident" while in holding.

I was screwed. I couldn't risk it. The cops couldn't be trusted.

Shit! For now, I'd follow Albert's plan and try to get out of this alive. Unzipping the backpack, I pulled out the suit I'd taken. *Voilà!* Complete transformation from casual islander to businessman.

I couldn't trust the cops or Albert. But Albert was a safer bet than a dirty cop.

26

Hoyt stood in the kitchen, his hands resting in hot, soapy dishwater. His gaze was pointed at the side yard, where a willow tree swayed in the wind. But his mind was somewhere else entirely.

"You know those dishes are never going to get clean like that."

He nearly jumped out of his skin when his wife spoke from behind him. Water sloshed out of the sink. Hoyt sighed at the mess and saw he was still holding the breakfast plate he'd been scrubbing.

"Shoot." Setting the clean plate aside, he started wiping the counter with the sponge, trying to push the water back into the sink.

"What's up, dear?"

"Nothing. I'm just..." He shrugged, then shook his shoulders. "I'm feeling itchy."

"Itchy?" Angie smirked, her gaze flicking downward. "You've been soaking your hands in dishwater for fifteen minutes now. If that's not cleared it up yet, maybe you should call the doc."

Hoyt's chuckle ended with a sigh. "Maybe."

"You're not itchy." Angie arched an eyebrow. "Though you may have dishpan hands from your dishwashing style. But you're definitely jumpier than a long-tailed cat in a room full of rocking chairs, as Mama says."

"More like a dog before a thunderstorm." Hoyt blew out a deep breath, trying to figure out why he felt so uneasy. The last time he'd felt this way had been the morning before Hurricane Boris made landfall. He glanced out the window, checking the sky. The few clouds were thin and harmless. It was a beautiful day to be off work.

Boomer, his elderly long-haired rough collie, was resting at his feet. She was so old, most of her colors had faded to a gray-and-white mix, but her devotion remained as strong as ever. Boomer huffed at his weather prediction, then rolled over to curl up closer to his feet.

"Pretty sure the storm is happening inside your head, dear. That dog has always been your emotional barometer." Angie leaned down and gave the collie a quick belly rub. "The more upset you are, the closer she gets to you. That's why she spent your entire recovery time jammed as close to the bed as she could get."

That was a fact Hoyt couldn't deny. Boomer hated sleeping on the bed, preferring the cooler floor to stretch out on. But for the first few days after getting back from having his ruptured appendix removed, she'd slept on the bed at his feet, keeping an eye on him. After that, she'd curled up on the floor, moving a bit farther away every day until she was back to her usual spot under the window.

He smiled down at his furry shadow, and she slapped her tail against the linoleum a few times. "Yeah. Dogs are great like that. You can always depend on them to tell your truths even when you can't or won't."

"So…" Angie prodded him in the side, making him twitch. "What are you feeling?"

"Like something's building." Hoyt rested the final dish on the drying rack. "There's something weird about this case we're working with the FBI. I can't believe a kid like Dillon Miller would be as good at robbing banks as he was. Also, who the hell decides that their first crime is going to be something as risky as robbing a bank?"

"Why do they think it was the Miller boy who did it?"

"His name's on the rental papers for the car that was used."

"Well, surely the name Dillon Miller isn't all that uncommon."

Hoyt pulled the plug on the sink before grabbing a hand towel. "It's not. I already thought of that and looked it up. There're several of them just in the Tidewater region. Also, as of the last time I checked the case file, there's no physical evidence connecting him to the car or the bank right now. We got a print from the house the bank robber broke into, but nothing to compare it to."

He dried his hands and sighed. "And we haven't tracked down where Dillon is either, but the evidence against him is circumstantial. With so many other twists to this case, it's unlikely he's our culprit."

"You want to go into work to prove he's innocent?" She crossed her arms.

"Yeah. But it's my day off. You know how Rebecca is about us taking time off. She wants us to have a chance to relax and recharge." His argument sounded lame, even to his own ears. A kid was facing federal charges, and he was old enough now to be tried as an adult. Even if Dillon was proven innocent later, the accusation could destroy his life.

"Exactly. You know she's right. Too bad she doesn't take

her own advice. Anyway, you have plenty of coworkers who are fully capable of doing the job. You can't tell me that Rebecca isn't already double-checking every single detail, making sure she's got all the evidence before moving forward. How many times have you told me how methodical and unbiased she is in her investigations?"

"More than I can remember." He hung the towel on its rod and turned to lean against the counter.

"Exactly. So if you have a concern, you can always send her a message letting her know. In the meantime, why don't you get out of the house? Didn't you say you had some errands you needed to run today? That'll help keep your mind off the case."

"What about you? You have any plans for the afternoon? If not, you know I always love your company, even if it's to the dry cleaners."

Resting her hands on his chest, Angie leaned forward to give him a quick peck on the lips. "I'm about to leave to go sit with Ryker. It's my turn today. He's still not fully recovered. At least, that's what the doctors say. To me, he seems perfectly fine."

"Seems like a long time to need a babysitter. From what I understand, he's been cleared to do pretty much everything." Getting out of the house did seem like a good plan. Hell, if Hoyt hurried, he might even be able to get his errands done in time to have lunch with Ryker and Angie.

"I think it's more likely that he's using some excuse so he can stay longer with Rebecca. But that might be the hopeless romantic in me." Angie pushed away and went to fetch her purse.

That sounded like something Ryker would do. "Tell you what, how about I swing by and see for myself how well he's doing once I get my errands done?"

"I like the sound of that." Angie kissed him goodbye. "And while you're chasing around town in your truck, you can listen to your work radio to stay updated on the case." Her eyes twinkled merrily at him, as if she knew she'd read his mind.

27

Rebecca was once again neck-deep in paperwork for the station remodel, checking over the plans for the new holding cells they were having installed. One cell might have been enough, but there was room in the budget for two. And floor space wasn't an issue if they were right next to each other.

But with the new additions, she also had to write up new standard operating procedures as well as emergency plans. In case of fire, flood, hurricane, the wrath of the Elder Ones —each scenario required step-by-step instructions.

When a sharp knock rattled her doorframe, she was more than happy to be interrupted. Benson's grinning face was a welcome sight.

"Thought you might like a little update on the case. The forensic reports aren't written up yet, but I got briefed a bit ago." He shifted his weight, and she could see Stalwart waiting patiently behind him, clutching a laptop.

"Yes. Please." Rebecca motioned to the barrel chairs set across from her desk, then continued the movement and pushed aside the last stack of paperwork. "I could use an excuse. I mean a break."

Benson stepped into her office—but before sitting, he carefully prodded the chairs and even checked his fingertips to make sure they hadn't been exposed to anything.

She smirked. "And they called *me* paranoid."

"You were never paranoid, West. I was just so good at getting you back no one else ever noticed." He carefully lowered himself onto the cushion, still ready to spring up in case anything happened.

"They never caught me either. I was way too sneaky for that." She rocked her head to the side and shrugged. "After the airhorn thing, at least. And don't worry about the chairs. I figured you'd call if you had an update." She looked over at Stalwart, indicating the second chair with her eyes.

Stalwart, who'd been curiously watching his SAC, shuffled into the room and sat down. He threw open his laptop, wiggling in his seat in apparent eagerness about the news.

"So what did the all-knowing FBI forensic lab find out for us?" Rebecca picked up a pen, ready to take notes.

Benson jerked his head decisively. "Nothing."

Rebecca blinked. Then blinked again as she tried to make sense of his statement. "Excuse me?"

"They found nothing. All over the car, inside and out."

"That's not good." She sat back in her chair and thought through those implications. For them to find nothing, there almost certainly was nothing to be found. Which meant the bank robber had used forensic countermeasures up to par with the brightest and most dedicated team of scientists the federal agency could hire.

Benson was studying her face. She was sure her expression reflected her every thought. "But when they found all that nothing, that made them suspicious. They checked handles, knobs, belts, everything. The entire car was wiped clean. When they pulled in the vacuum to collect lint, dust, and hair samples, all they found was a bit of pollen. It was from a loblolly pine."

That was something…

"On a hunch, I had them test the pollen, and it matched the loblolly pine on the edge of the parking lot. Since that was the only thing in the car we found, it's safe to say that the bank robber parked, got out, then did a full cleanup job while wearing protective equipment."

"Which doesn't sound like an eighteen-year-old kid with a spotless criminal record to me." Rebecca watched Benson like a hawk, but there wasn't a single twitch or shift to give away his thoughts or feelings. She was more than a little bit jealous of his poker face.

"That's what we thought too. Thankfully, this guy wasn't as meticulous at the Longfellow house. In fact, he left evidence all over the place."

"He probably just hadn't had a chance to clean up. He was surprised and booked it."

"We're working to date everything we've found, considering the blood in the foyer predates the bank robbery. They're also still working to separate the blood samples from the polyurethane and wood flooring, but those prints your man Frost lifted got us a hit."

Stalwart was damn near bouncing in his seat. Benson waved for him to go ahead.

"We found a strong match. His name is Hudson Buchanon, twenty-two years old, from Black Creek, North Carolina."

"That's great news." Rebecca's relief that the prints didn't belong to Dillon was immense. "Have you already picked him up?"

Benson shook his head. "We don't have him in custody yet. But I've got my people gearing up to bring him in while we pull warrants. We'll get one for his arrest and another for his financials to track his movements."

"Unless he's been using the cash he stole to finance his expenses."

Benson gave the briefest nod of agreement. "Also, the fingerprints point to him being a squatter, nothing worse. That's not going to be enough to get an arrest warrant, no matter how much we suspect he's the robber. Yeah, the bank bags were in the house as well. But to charge him with a bank robbery, we need something more substantial than proving he was, at some point, in the same abandoned house as the bags."

Stalwart looked like he was going to shatter into a million pieces if he didn't get to finish talking. Rebecca took pity on him this time and asked the question she knew he had to be waiting for.

"What do we know about Hudson Buchanon?"

"We were able to match his fingerprints so fast because I was certain I recognized his modus operandi from a bank robbery a few months back that, in fact, he was charged with. You see, I like to keep up to date with open cases, and this was one of them. With that, I asked forensics to compare the print we pulled from the house to the prints from the other robbery and got a match from his booking." Stalwart nodded in a perfect imitation of a bobblehead. "In the previous case, a small-town bank in Sheffield, Virginia was robbed by a man wearing a full gorilla suit and black gloves."

Rebecca opened her mouth to ask a follow-up question, but Stalwart was unstoppable now that he'd been given full rein to talk about his findings.

"In that case, Buchanon did many of the same things as he did here. He got all the money from the tills while holding the manager at gunpoint. During the robbery, he systematically trashed the lobby and any desks he could get his gloved hands on. Once he had all the money in bags, he put the bank bags in his own bag. Then he had the manager tape the hands of all the staff behind their backs while lying on their stomachs in a closet."

She nodded and once again opened her mouth, but Benson gave her a tiny shake of his head. She linked her fingers together and gave Stalwart her full attention.

"Compared to the first case, the main difference is that the previous manager was bound and left with his staff. The forensic countermeasures were so good, we were unable to pull any evidence from the scene. It was too cluttered with old DNA, fingerprints, dust, and crushed candies that the bank kept in little bowls around the lobby. His M.O. also matched six other bank robberies. All about six months apart. Each one in a different small town in Virginia or North Carolina."

Stalwart took a breath before continuing.

"The only solid evidence we had linking Hudson Buchanon to the robbery in Sheffield was a piece of video surveillance from a neighboring store that caught him pulling off his gorilla mask while driving away. We got the make and model of the car, but the original video was fuzzy. Before we could get it to the techs to refine the image, the original video was corrupted. So without any corroborating evidence, the case against him didn't hold up."

"Corrupted how?" Rebecca asked.

Stalwart shrugged. "Could be the tape itself was re-recorded so many times it failed. Could be someone took a magnet to it—"

"Someone could've tampered with evidence?"

"I mean, I'm just speculating. I don't know for sure."

Benson made his own observations. "His general height and body type matched what could be presumed to fit inside the costume, but as you know, that's circumstantial at best."

Stalwart gave his boss the stink eye and launched ahead. "Luckily, a state trooper, a Trooper Dolph Burke, actually just brought in a picture he obtained of Hudson taking off the gorilla disguise while driving. He said he was going through a folder for a different case and found it misfiled. Having this will help link him to the previous case as well as this one."

A queasy feeling twisted Rebecca's stomach. State Trooper Dolph Burke, the very same man who was gunning for sheriff, according to Dick Vale. He had a tendency to abandon his post and yell a lot. It wouldn't surprise her if Burke himself had incompetently misfiled the original photograph and then tried to cover his tracks.

Not that she could prove it.

Again, Benson spoke while Stalwart took a breath. "We must consider that this could be a copycat, as the M.O. doesn't completely match. Hudson has never used violence before."

Rebecca waited a beat to see if either man was going to continue, but they seemed to finally be out of pertinent information. Stalwart might be a squirrely dude, but he was top-notch with his research skills. "Or he could be evolving his methods after being caught once. Getting off due to sheer luck might have scared him into being more careful."

"Or he could want to change up his M.O. a bit, so he's not linked to the other crimes. After all, he doesn't know we have that new photo Burke found." Benson steepled his fingers, tapping them together. "He hasn't used violence against any of the people before. It was always directed at inanimate objects. As far as we know, he's also never hung around town after committing his crimes, like he did this time at the Longfellow home."

"So to your knowledge," Rebecca punched Hudson Buchanon's name into the computer to see what other information they might have on him, "his M.O. is pretty simple." She found the name that matched with the proper city and got her first sight of the man.

He was twenty-two years old, thin and lanky, as if he hadn't grown into his adult body yet. His hair was dark and a bit curly, hanging down past his shoulders like an overgrown bush, while his face was clean-shaven.

If she didn't look too closely, she could see how he could be mistaken for Dillon Miller. Both had a young, awkward basketball-player build and similar hair color.

"I'll send his picture along with a BOLO to my people so we can keep an eye out for him. You might want to question the drivers for the bus that runs from Coastal Ridge to here as well. There was a bus stop not far from where he ditched his getaway car."

Benson nodded. "We'll check ride shares too."

Rebecca stared at the young face. "I still find it incredibly strange that he used an ID with Dillon Miller at the rental agency and stayed in Mitchell Longfellow's house."

"That could be part of his M.O. too. We never found a car linked to a local before. However, with every bank he's robbed, he seems to know the layout. We don't know how long he might have been in town, scoping out the bank. He could have heard about the Longfellow house being vacant or heard Dillon's name around town and decided to use it. Our case against Hudson didn't go very far, and we handed it over to the Sheffield authorities once they had that video footage, trusting they would follow up on the case."

While that could be true, Rebecca thought the only thing Longfellow and Dillon had in common, other than being locals, was the Yacht Club. And when you lived in a sparsely populated town, pretty much every islander would be connected to the Yacht Club through six degrees of separation or fewer. It wasn't the first time Dillon Miller had tangled with those terrible men.

Longfellow had been a hired stooge who'd probably been doing their bidding for years, while Dillon's life had been collateral damage for their debauchery.

Stalwart double-checked with Benson, pinching his lips momentarily as the eagerness began to ebb. He probably thought she wouldn't notice, but Rebecca had excellent powers of observation. Benson got up and closed the office door, making both her eyebrows jump.

Immediately, she was transported to her days as a rookie under Benson's tutelage. The only time she'd seen him do something similar was when he was about to chew her out. But she hadn't done anything wrong in this case. Nor was she his subordinate.

The analyst's fingers tapped a nervous beat on his laptop. "I dug up some other information for you…not related to the case."

28

"I looked into the guy who's trying to buy your house."

Rebecca straightened in her ergonomic office chair. She hadn't been sure what to expect when Benson closed the door, but talking about a personal matter certainly hadn't been on her list of possibilities. She shifted her gaze to Stalwart.

"This whole situation seemed too odd to ignore. Some corrupt treasurer attempted to raise the taxes on a town sheriff's rental without any legal basis. It was as if he was targeting you. Then, when you thought everything was settled and you could stay in your home, an unexpected millionaire shows up out of nowhere wanting to buy it. It makes no sense." The analyst shook his head in disbelief.

Benson resumed his seat. "I highly doubt this was a coincidence. For that reason, I asked Stalwart to investigate and see if there might've been something unique about the dwelling which you were unaware of."

Stalwart once again checked with his supervisor, who waved for him to proceed. "The person trying to purchase is Claude Bennet. He's an importer-exporter with personal wealth in the millions. There's no reason a man as rich as him should want to buy your rental." He spun the laptop around, showing the real estate listing Deborah had put up.

"While you and the current owner seem to care a great deal about the property, as far as I can tell, there's nothing special or noteworthy about the house itself. We've dug into the history of the land and house, and even investigated current and future development prospects in the area. There's simply nothing there that could entice someone like him to pay so much in excess of its value."

Benson sat back in his chair. "Which raises the question, why does Claude Bennet want your house so badly?"

"Does he have any connections to the island?" The paranoid side of Rebecca's mind jumped to the idea that this could be yet another Yacht Club scheme. She'd seen them pull something similar with the Alton property and the old lighthouse. "Personal or business."

"He has business ties with several wealthy families that have homes on Shadow Island and yachts docked at your Seaview Marina." Stalwart glanced between her and his boss.

Benson watched her intently. Her face had to be giving away all her unease. With every new thing she learned, it seemed more and more likely that the Aqua Mafia was trying to get rid of her by taking away her house—the reason she'd come to this island in the first place.

However, saying all that out loud, explaining what she thought was happening, would make her look like a lunatic seeing conspiracies where there weren't any. She knew there were plenty of stories exactly like that circling around inside the FBI.

The rumor mill in the federal agency wasn't anywhere as efficient as the one on Shadow Island, but it took longer for the blather to be discarded even after it was disproven. For now, she didn't want to say anything that might make Stalwart—or worse, Benson—believe any of the rumors.

"Maybe his business ties are why he's so desperate to get a house on the island." She tried to shrug casually.

"If it was because of his business links, then it would make more sense for him to get a house in the same neighborhood as the people he'd be dealing with." Stalwart shook his head. "No, the only thing that makes sense is that there's something in this particular house that he wants."

Rebecca had to agree with that. Her fear was that what Claude Bennet wanted was her.

29

The car was at the edge of the parking lot of the public beach, right where Albert said it would be. A white Kia Rio, fairly newish from the look of it. I walked up beside it, on the passenger side, and glanced in. Keys dangled from the ignition. It was ready to go.

I walked past it and up to the sidewalk. After everything I'd gone through over the last couple of days, I didn't trust the people providing the vehicle. Ignoring the car completely, I meandered to the other end of the lot. An older couple walked hand in hand along the beach, watching the ocean. It appeared that the thin gentleman noticed me and said something to the woman.

Probably my imagination. At the far end of the lot, I peered out, pretending to be searching for someone.

Except I wasn't pretending at all. I was looking for someone, but no one specific. After all, they'd said Longfellow's house would be a safe place to lay low 'til my ride arrived. That had backfired, nearly getting me caught. I wasn't going to be so trusting a second time.

Turning on my heel, I retraced my path, trying to get a

better view of the getaway car the Yacht Club had procured. There had to be something wrong with it. Something I was missing. Maybe a bomb strapped to the bottom just waiting for me to turn the key in the ignition.

I was living proof that these "businessmen" hired crooks and criminals to handle all kinds of tasks for them. Of course they could tamper with the car. I needed to inspect it as casually as I could. Stepping off the sidewalk, I moved through the lot, trying to see the vehicle from a different angle. The whole time, I kept an eye out for anyone in the area who might be watching me.

A couple of moms with young children climbed out of a minivan while trying to balance everything they needed for a day at the beach. Three toddlers whined and fussed as the women unloaded the gear. The moms were already frustrated with the antsy kids and were probably tempted to scrap the whole outing. Other than a quick, disinterested glance at me, they ignored me. The toddlers, at least, I was certain weren't here as spies.

That couple was still on the beach. The woman was kneeling in the sand, digging something up, while the man watched her. He was smiling. Did the woman just glance at me? Or maybe the rowdy kids in the parking lot got her attention.

Though the couple seemed innocent enough, something in my gut made me wary.

Were they watching me? I turned a slow circle, keeping up the act of waiting for someone. The woman had sandy-blond hair, gone mostly white and silver. Both sported deep tans that made me think they were locals. The man was way thin. His jeans were basic. Neither of them wore ostentatious jewelry—at least, there was nothing gaudy I could see from this distance.

That was a good hint that they weren't Yacht Club. Every

member I'd met had some visible bling. Albert had been slathered in rings and worn a tie bar with a diamond on it that matched his cufflinks. His watch probably cost more than the house I was hoping to buy one day.

This whole situation was suspicious. I couldn't risk blindly following Albert's orders like a good boy. There was no plausible reason for the older couple to still be there so close to the parking lot. Digging in the sand seemed to be a ploy to linger. It made me uneasy. More than fifteen minutes had passed. They should've moved on by now.

The whole thing stank of one of those stings you see going sideways online.

With a frustrated shake of my head, I sighed. The moms with their kids had caught up to me, so my act was mostly for the sake of keeping up my disguise of a businessman waiting for someone. Neither woman spared me a glance as they herded the three children toward their beach excursion.

Decision time. Should I take the car or find my own way out of town? Trust the Yacht Club or my own two feet?

Whatever happened, I wasn't uploading the virus on the thumb drive in my bag.

I wanted to cut and run. All I needed was my money and the freedom it granted me.

Stepping past the women and their excited children, I moved through the parking lot, away from the Kia.

"Miss Vera! Miss Vera!"

"Mister Jim!"

The joyous shrieks of the three kids rang out through the parking lot as they took off running toward the sand.

"Oh, you made it! Miss Vera has found some pretty shells. Would you like to come see them?" The old skinny dude greeted the children.

I paused. Of course. The old couple had actually been

waiting for someone. No one had been watching me. It was all in my imagination.

Feeling foolish for nearly walking away from a good thing, I turned back to the car. I opened the door, still ready to scram if things turned bad.

No alarms went off.

No police came running.

I tossed the backpack in before dropping into the driver's seat.

I slammed the door shut and turned the keys in the ignition, and the engine purred to life. Nothing exploded. Things were starting to look up. The engine sounded weak yet steady. This car was probably only a four-cylinder at best.

So long as it got me to where I needed to go, I didn't care. A wimpy little car like this wouldn't attract any police attention, so that was key.

It was perfect.

Releasing a relieved breath, I put it in reverse and backed out. The last few days had messed with my nerves, making me see conspiracies where there were none.

As I pulled onto the road, I glanced at the dash. The gas tank was nearly empty.

Of course they'd still find some way to screw things up. The Yacht Club needed to get their act together.

I wouldn't be able to make it to Coastal Ridge, even with good gas mileage.

There were plenty of gas stations in town, but the place was swarming with law enforcement. I again considered leaving the car behind.

But it wouldn't take that long to gas up.

And a full tank meant I could stay on the road and leave this forsaken island.

30

Rebecca leaned against the kitchenette folding table, sipping her coffee. Benson's team had let her know they'd checked out Buchanon's house in North Carolina without making it obvious. Mail was piled up so high in the wall-mounted mailbox that it was spilling onto the porch. The grass had grown long, and there were drifts of leaves collecting around the tires of his car.

There was every indication that Hudson Buchanon had not been home for at least a couple weeks. Hearing that, Benson had left to meet up with the rest of his team before they made entry. Stalwart had holed himself up in her office with his computer. With everything on her mind from what they'd told her about her house and the man that was trying to buy it, Rebecca had wandered out to the bullpen.

She stared at the back of Jake's head while he worked. He was currently writing a report from his patrol. Though half a stack of paperwork still needed her attention, going out on a patrol sounded like a much better option.

Jake can hold down the fort. And Meg and Dale have both been saying that I need to get out more. Be seen by the voters so they realize I'm "on the job."

While she knew that Wallace had been one to make his presence known by always hanging out in public, basing her actions on a corrupt but well-intentioned sheriff was probably not the best idea. The Aqua Mafia had used all their political pull to make sure Wallace had won every election. That had been achieved by ensuring he ran unopposed.

Rebecca rubbed the bridge of her nose. She wasn't cut out for political games. Half the time, she worried she was overthinking. The other times, she worried she wasn't thinking about it enough.

Just like now.

Should she stay or should she go now? The lyrics from The Clash's song immediately got stuck in her head, and she sighed.

"You all right back there, Boss?"

Rebecca dropped her hand and saw Jake had turned around in his chair.

"Yeah. Too much paperwork and now I've got a song stuck in my head." She straightened, pushing her shoulders back, intent on making a decision. "I'm going to do a quick patrol before grabbing lunch. That'll give my brain time to rest before I have to wade through all that red tape."

Jake shook his head. "This is why I never bothered to take any of the tests for promotions." He gestured at his computer. "The paperwork I have to do now is more than enough for me. I don't want to have to deal with the mountains of it that come with moving up the ranks."

"I completely understand that sentiment. When I arrived here, I was a tourist. Paperwork wasn't even on my radar. One case turned that all on its head." Rebecca chuckled, thinking back to how the people of Shadow Island had needed her. And the deputies had needed someone to lead them. So she had stayed to fill that role. "When Wallace died, someone had to do this job. And Deputy Frost flat out refused."

"No shit?" Jake stared at her as if he didn't believe her.

It was hard for her to wrap her mind around, too, and she'd been there for the entire argument. "No shit. You think things are hectic now? This past summer was even worse."

"I remember the missing girls and the leech-covered deranged psycho who 'beat your head in.'" Jake smirked, humor dancing in his ice-blue eyes.

Rebecca rolled her eyes. She had slammed into a hunk of wood in the old, rotting carcass of a ship while trying to dodge the leech- and feces-covered psycho, Kevin Garland. If he'd bashed her head in, she wouldn't have survived.

Jake had been the state trooper who'd refused to take her statement while she was severely concussed. He'd followed her to the hospital but waited until she was home recovering to question her.

She wasn't certain, but she might have puked on Jake's shoes due to that concussion. He'd been too much of a gentleman to add that to the official report, however. Also absent from it was how she'd needed to wear Darian Hudson's deputy hat to cover her eyes so she could stop getting sick.

A pang of loss ran through her like it always did when she thought of the kind, virtuous Army soldier-turned-deputy. She sighed, realizing she'd forgotten all the things that had been bothering her for the last hour while talking with Jake. Her second-guessing melted when she turned her mind to what she'd already accomplished as sheriff and the relationships she'd built.

"Right. I'm going to head out to lunch, then patrol. Hold down the fort—"

"Uh, Sheriff?" Elliot swiveled in his chair at the reception desk, leaning over to talk to them. "I've got a report of a stolen car. A white 2018 Kia Rio, plate is Victor Romeo X-ray seven six nine six. The man who stole it is a white male about six-three or six-four, short, bleached blond hair, and with a brown beard and mustache. The caller described him as being in his early twenties with a thin build. He's wearing a loose, dark-gray business suit with black sneakers and carrying a dark Rockport bag. She also thinks he had a gun. The car was taken from the number four public access lot and was last seen heading north."

Rebecca blinked in surprise and Jake cocked his head. "That's an exceptionally detailed description. Is it the owner who called it in?" She was already walking toward the door as Jake started gathering his things.

"No. According to the caller, an older woman from the sound of it, she saw him break into the car in the parking lot and take off." Elliot spun around and picked up the pad he'd written the information on. "She didn't tell me her name, though."

Car theft wasn't something they usually had to deal with. In fact, this was the first reported car theft since Rebecca had become sheriff. She'd only seen a handful in all the reports Wallace had filed over the years. And she'd spent plenty of time going through those files.

A car theft while a bank robber might still be hanging around their town. It was too coincidental. As Benedict Cumberbatch's Sherlock Holmes observed, *The universe is rarely so lazy*.

"Send out a BOLO on it, Elliot, and alert Coastal Ridge. Jake, head to the bridge and hang out in that area. The best part about being on an island with only one road in and out is being able to pin criminals down. At least he didn't steal a boat."

Rebecca finished gearing up. "Call me if you see the Kia.

I'm going to head down Main Street, over to the public access lot, and work my way around." She leaned down the hall and hollered for Stalwart.

"You think it's the bank robber." Jake shoved his gun into his belt and grabbed his hat.

"So do you." Rebecca checked her sidearm out of habit. "And remember, if it is him, he's armed and already proven he's willing to kill. Be careful out there."

Jake dipped his head. "You too."

She turned for the briefest moment as she passed Dispatch on her way out the door. "Oh, and Elliot? See what happens when you say the Q word?"

31

Rebecca slid through traffic, the little bit there was of it. Lunchtime had passed, and it was a weekday, so almost everyone was either at work or school. Traffic really only consisted of a few cars, which made keeping an eye out for the stolen Kia Rio even easier. A white car would be easy to spot.

Stalwart sat in the passenger seat, searching every crossroad they passed while clutching his phone like a lifeline. "You sure do have a lot happening in your small town. Much more than most towns this size."

That was the understatement of the century, and a theme Benson had been repeating since he arrived.

The last time Stalwart had ridden out with her team, he'd been dragged into a shootout with a trio of human traffickers and three traumatized little girls. Granted, by the time he'd shown up, Rebecca had taken down two of them and was negotiating with the third for the safe release of the kidnapped children.

"There's a lot going on in this town." She rolled to a stop

at a stop sign while returning a nod from a man walking down the street.

"Do you know him?"

"Nope. I've seen him around before, but I don't know his name. I think it's more that they're waving to the sheriff's car than to Sheriff Rebecca West."

"Small town pleasantries." Stalwart went back to searching the streets for any sign of the stolen vehicle. "It's very much like *The Andy Griffith Show*."

"An idyllic little place set in the sixties." Rebecca had gotten so used to the town from the perspective of a law enforcement officer that she'd slowly stopped seeing it the way she had as a child. The perfect, quaint little beach setting where there were always smiling faces, plenty of sunshine, and a never-ending assortment of shells to collect.

She looked at it now and saw the fresh paint on Hugh's surf shop, but knew it was hiding storm damage. The road they were on was the same one a dazed, blood-covered man had walked down while muttering about dead mermaids.

Even the lighthouse, which she could barely make out over the canopy of trees in the distance, now had a dark memory associated with it. It had been used to hold a handful of Historical Society members hostage.

"This is the tourist-friendly face of Shadow Island you're seeing. There's a lot of deep, dark, and twisted layers underneath, though." She waved to a little girl in pigtails with a bandage on her knee who was staring at her with something akin to hero worship. The little one didn't manage to work up the courage to wave back before Rebecca pulled away from the stop and continued to the lot where the car had been stolen.

"I get that." Stalwart shifted uncomfortably in his seat, adjusting his seat belt. Rebecca hadn't bothered putting hers on, knowing she might have to bail out of her cruiser at any time. "I might not be a field agent or a special agent, but I'm not sheltered. What I've found in my research is much worse than what I saw the last time I worked with you. Girls, children, who we weren't able to save before they were sold."

Rebecca softened toward him. She knew all too well what he was talking about. She'd also worked on cases where the bodies were never found. The ones involving children always hit the hardest.

"But usually you don't have so many different types of violent crimes all happening in one place like you do here." He kept his face turned away from her. "It's statistically unlikely, given what I know of the area."

What Stalwart didn't know about Shadow Island and its inhabitants could fill a book. Maybe even twenty. Hell, Rebecca had been digging into the history of it, reading through old reports, talking with people, and researching the residents and businesses—and she still had only scratched the surface.

When she didn't respond, Stalwart turned to her. "How deep does it go?"

She had to think about that. Really, truly think about it. How deep *did* this go? Rebecca didn't know, and that worried her. In fact, that same question kept her up some nights as she tried to come up with an answer.

"You can't believe that way-too-detailed stolen car report was any more of a coincidence than the fact that your real estate agent was supposed to show up at the house that a bank robber had chosen as a hideaway. In fact, both coincidences seem to be well timed and intentional." Stalwart glanced at a passing white minivan. "Someone is directing all this, and I want to know what's going on."

"I don't know." Rebecca hated saying that phrase. Especially when it was about something as important as this.

They were searching for an armed man who, by any

reasonable line of thinking, should've been long gone by now. While there was the slightest chance that Hudson Buchanon was not the same man who'd stolen the vehicle today—the description didn't match except for height, age, and build, the things someone couldn't change about their own appearance—she didn't believe that. And clearly neither did Stalwart.

He was staring at her with narrowed eyes, chewing on his lower lip.

"I honestly don't." Rebecca repeated the hateful phrase. "I've only been here three months. Every time I think I've gotten to the bottom of things, I find yet another layer below that one. Then another. But I agree with you. There seems to be more to this case than a man who wants to get rich quick robbing banks. What this bank robbery has to do with everything else I've managed to put together, I couldn't tell you. Not for certain, at least."

Stalwart's left eye twitched as his fingers drummed along the door panel. "Not certain? Does that mean you have some theories?"

"'Theories' might be too solid of a word for what I have. I have suppositions. Rumors. Conjecture. Some facts. More assumptions than I'm comfortable with. A list of names. And more than a hundred cases, which might or might not be related. All of it held together with guesswork and speculation."

Rebecca nearly smiled, knowing that was precisely the kind of broad collection of information that analysts like Stalwart thrived on.

"I could help."

She wished he could, but they had a bank robber to find. "None of it is simple enough for me to even begin to explain right now."

As she'd imagined, Stalwart was on the edge of his seat

with anticipation, eager to find the links that might tie everything together. Which might be exactly what she needed. After all, he was a data analyst and might see connections she'd missed.

"Once we get this case put to rest, and I can find some time, I'll sit down and explain everything I know to you and Benson." He was beaming like a child who'd been told Santa was coming. "Most of these cases would end up with the FBI anyway. Maybe with your help, we can get them there faster."

Faster, and hopefully with a smaller body count than without their assistance.

32

Deputy Frost hung the metal hangers with his clean uniforms on the hook over the left rear passenger door. Picking up his laundry was the final thing he'd needed to get done. He'd taken too long with his errands and had missed lunch with Angie and Ryker.

His heavy sense of anxiety from earlier had told him to listen to the police scanner, so he'd had it on the whole time he'd been out running errands. While cell phones were certainly handy, he preferred the dash-mounted radio for emergencies. He could also use it to listen to his coworkers on his time off. So far, it had been silent.

As he got behind the wheel, Elliot's voice filled the cab of his truck.

"All officers, be on the lookout for a 2018 white Kia Rio, license plate Victor Romeo X-ray seven six nine six. Suspect is a white male, six-three or four, short, bleached blond hair with a brown beard and mustache, wearing a dark-gray business suit, black sneakers, and a Rockport backpack. Possibly armed."

"Shit, all that information and they didn't hand us the suspect's middle name too?" Hoyt twisted in his seat, backing out of the parking spot. He was already on the north side of the island. Which meant it wouldn't take much effort to check the roads on his way home.

"Dispatch, this is Frost. I'm on Coastal Drive, south of the library, in my personal vehicle. I'll swing down the west side of the area and keep an eye out for that BOLO."

"Deputy Frost, isn't today your day off, sir?"

Sir. That wasn't something he'd been called at work for quite some time. "It is. That's why I'm in my personal truck. I can still keep my eyes open for a Kia Rio and let you know if I see anything." Hoyt slowed down to just under the speed limit while sweeping his gaze left and right.

Rebecca's voice came back to him. "Sounds good, Deputy Frost. I'm on Main, heading south now. I'll stick to the east side of the island. Deputy Coffey is covering the bridge and surrounding area while Coastal's been notified to watch the other side. We'll catch this guy in no time."

He was certain that was true.

It was after lunch but before school let out. The traffic was fairly light, and it was a sunny day. A white Rio? Hoyt was amused that anyone would even bother stealing a car with a small engine. They had no real oomph, as Angie called it.

As he passed the turnoff for the bridge, he noticed a cruiser pulling onto the shoulder right before it. That had to be Jake, getting into position. The bridge was one of the main reasons no one with a brain would risk stealing a car. They were on an island. Unless they could get the car over the bridge before the car was reported missing, they were pretty much stuck.

The description said it was a young businessman, though —not your average car thief. Young, sure. Male, almost always. Wearing a business suit at a beach parking lot? Not so much. That would make them stand out like a whore in church.

Or it would be the next weird occurrence in a string of weird things that had been happening for the last several days. All of which were tied to that bank robbery. The anxiety sent Hoyt's stomach lurching again.

A storm isn't about to hit. It's me, waiting for the other shoe to drop in this convoluted case. That's why I've been on edge all day.

As that realization struck, Hoyt spotted a flash of white next to the Stop & Save gas station on his left. A white Kia Rio had turned into the parking lot from the side entrance and was pulling up next to a pump.

The nose of the car was facing him. Fortunately, Virginia required plates on the front as well as the back, so it only took a moment for him to be able to read *VRX-7696*.

"Dispatch, this is Deputy Frost. I've spotted the stolen Kia Rio." Hoyt pulled into the turn lane and let a car pass while he waited for the driver of the stolen vehicle to get out. "I'm at the Stop and Save on Coastal Drive."

"Deputy Frost, be advised the driver might be armed." Elliot's response was immediate.

"Copy that. Again, I'm in my personal vehicle and in civilian clothes. Boss knows what I drive, but Coffey, be advised, it's a red GMC Sierra extended cab. It doesn't need any additional holes in it."

"Copy that, Frost. Since it's a GMC, I can't imagine it would pose any kind of threat to me so long as I don't get behind the wheel. I'll refrain from shooting it. I'll be there in two minutes."

Hoyt's pride took a hit with Coffey's harsh words against his old girl, joke or not. He pulled into the gas station parking lot. Other than the Kia, there was a Volkswagen

Beetle parked at a pump. He looped around the lot to get a better look at the Kia driver.

Peering through his dry cleaning, Hoyt could tell the driver was a man in a business suit, his hair bleached blond. Unfortunately, the man's face was obscured as he leaned in through the driver's door.

As he rolled past the pumps, Rebecca came on the line. "I don't have a lot of experience with petty car thefts. But isn't it mighty strange that a car thief would steal a car that needed gas and immediately stop to fuel up? I mean, the car he stole couldn't make it even the few miles to cross the bridge and away from the scene of the crime?"

"Most car thieves are stupid, Boss. Don't forget that aspect." Hoyt held the radio low, careful not to give himself away.

"Think you can get a picture of his face? Stalwart and I will be there in about three minutes."

"Yeah, Boss." Hoyt pulled into the pump a bay over from the Kia, orienting his vehicle the same direction. Before he got close, he turned his radio all the way down so it couldn't be overheard. He picked up his phone and casually swiped at it while opening his camera app. Making sure the flash was turned off, he snapped a photo as the man stood up and started to swing the door closed.

The car thief must've been on high alert already. His head jerked up, and he peered around.

Hoyt didn't react, pretending to be engrossed in his screen. He even moved his thumbs to mimic typing. It was a game of cat and mouse suddenly, with Hoyt forced to stay calm and not give any sign that he was more than just a regular Joe needing to fill his tank.

He put the truck in park as the other driver glanced over. Hoyt kept his eyes on his screen. Switching to the video app, he could watch the man without having to look at him out the truck's window. Having video footage was a bonus.

Slowly, the man relaxed. His eyes drifted away as he turned to the convenience store. The pumps only accepted credit or debit cards, so if the man intended to use cash, he would need to go inside to pay with his stolen bank money.

Perfect. I can wait. That gives Rebecca and Jake time to get here. Then, when the suspect gets back to his car, we can grab him as he's pumping gas.

Unhooking his belt, Hoyt was about to get out when the suspect's head swiveled around, shock painting his face. Snatching up the messenger bag from inside the car, the man took off running.

"What the hell?" Noticing where the man's attention had been focused, Hoyt cursed.

His dry-cleaned uniform hung in the back passenger window, on full display.

He turned up the radio, no longer needing to sneak around.

"Keep your head down. I'm worried this might be the same guy who robbed the bank. I repeat, Frost, keep your head down." Rebecca's voice droned as if she'd been saying that for a while now.

"Too late. I've been spotted." Hoyt kept an eye on his rearview mirror as the thief raced inside the gas station. "Suspect has entered the building. And I think you're right about him being the bank thief."

Before the doors had even closed, an entire display of snack cakes was strewn across the floor. Screams rang out after that.

Hoyt kept cursing to himself as he realized there were two other cars in the parking lot, and he didn't see anyone else at the pumps.

He jumped out of the truck, thanking his earlier anxiety

for forcing him to prepare for the worst as he pulled his concealed carry gun from the holster at his back. Blinds were being jerked over the windows as the thief raced along the front wall.

"Boss, I'm afraid I've sparked a hostage situation."

33

Rebecca revved the engine as she took her SUV over the grassy median and shuddered to a stop in the parking area between Hoyt's truck and the building. His vehicle was a basic civilian model and would be shredded if bullets started flying. Hers at least had bullet-resistant door panels. It would give them a tiny bit of protection. She threw her door open and slid out as Hoyt ran over to meet her.

According to forensic results, Buchanon had shot Arthur Carson with a 9mm. If this was the same man using the same weapon, her door could stop it no problem. The issue was, he'd had plenty of time to restock with new guns, or he might have a backup gun of a higher caliber. As always, it was best to play it safe and expect anything shy of a shoulder-mounted rocket launcher. Hoyt would've mentioned if he'd seen that.

Jake had left his post at the bridge and was parked sideways in the front entrance for the business, blocking anyone from pulling in on that side.

"Frost, move your truck to the side entrance. Do it fast and keep your head down." She spun around and saw that

Stalwart was doing the proper thing and not exiting via his passenger door—the side of the vehicle nearest the danger. Instead, he was crawling over the center console to reach the driver's door. "Have dispatch send all hands over. And tell CRPD what we've got going on over here in case he manages to make a run for it."

Leaving his lights going, Jake ran over to join them, standing at Rebecca's back and waiting for orders.

Hoyt turned, hopped in his GMC, and drove off as directed.

"Our team is hours away by now!" Stalwart spluttered and fumbled as he picked up the radio.

Rebecca pinned him in place with her glare. "Mine is here and more than capable of handling this, whether it's Hudson Buchanon or someone else." She gestured over her shoulder to Deputies Greg Abner and Trent Locke, jogging up behind her. They were both dressed in civilian clothes. Rebecca spotted Greg's vehicle parked on the shoulder of the road, hazard lights flashing.

"Hey, Boss. We were coming back from the range and heard the commotion." Greg waggled his handheld radio at her.

"Did you take that home with you?" Rebecca shook her head in amusement.

Jake snorted but said nothing.

Greg huffed in annoyance. "No, of course not. I bought it at Radio Shack twenty years ago, and it still works great. It gets left in the car. I don't mind helping out when I'm off duty. What do we have here? Frost said something about a hostage situation."

"We're still setting up the perimeter, so I'm not positive yet." Rebecca glanced over as Hoyt ran to join them. He was pulling on his vest over his loud Hawaiian shirt—the one with the flamingos Angie bought for him—at the same time. His hat was jammed on his head.

"The guy from the BOLO description had pulled into the station, gotten out, and was messing around in his car." Hoyt's cheeks reddened slightly. "Then he saw my uniform hanging in the back and ran inside. I figured he'd run straight through or try to hide, 'til he started pulling the blinds."

"Probably to protect his eyes from the glare of that shirt." Rebecca couldn't resist giving him a hard time. She herself kept a uniform in her truck. And another at the station. And a third in the back of her cruiser. It was always a good idea to be prepared for times just like this.

Hoyt ignored her. "It's been weirdly quiet."

Viviane pulled up in her Dodge Grand Caravan minivan. Keeping her head down, she sprinted over to join them, uniform hat in hand but otherwise in her civilian tank top and ripped jeans.

Hoyt was shaking his head. "Sorry, Boss. I forgot my uniform was back there." He dug his phone out of the pocket of his cargo shorts. "I got the picture you wanted, though."

Everyone's phones pinged as he texted the photo to them so they wouldn't have to huddle together and make targets of themselves.

Rebecca enlarged the image. The general appearance of the car thief matched the description that had been called in. More importantly, the cell image matched the face in Trooper Burke's photo of the bank robber, albeit with a dye job, haircut, and new facial hair. "This is our bank robber. And the person who left a fingerprint at the Longfellow's house...the squatter. It's the same guy."

"What the hell?" Hoyt took a closer look at the image on his phone. "What's this guy playing at? Is he staying on the island, trying to give us a hard time?" He jerked his head toward Rebecca's SUV. "Locke, you need something to mark you as a deputy on first sight. Go grab a vest. And get one for Abner and Darby too." He pointed his finger and drew a large circle around them. "We're about to get a lot of nosy people, including staties. We don't want friendly fire happening if they see you brandishing."

With these magic words, the deputies found their badges in a hurry, pinning them to belts or wearing them on lanyards.

"Boss." Greg ignored the chatter happening around him. His badge had been hanging from his neck the whole time. He pointed at the lime-green Focus parked at the side of the gas station. "I think I might know who's working inside. Lemme make some phone calls."

Rebecca nodded. "Take it to the side, though. Locke, you and Jake go around the left-hand side. We know this guy likes going out back doors. But don't lose sight of each other. He's already shown he's willing to kill. We'll go up and make contact. Darby, I've got a spare top in my trunk."

"I know where." Viviane opened the back of the SUV and pulled out Rebecca's go bag. Rebecca pulled her vest on over her uniform and tightened her utility belt at her waist.

"Stalwart, make sure the incoming troopers know not all my people are in full uniform." She cast a quick glance at Hoyt's shirt. "You're a walking target, Frost. Grab your shirt from the truck."

"Hey, I was trying to be cheerful," he retorted, but he retreated to retrieve his shirt.

Rebecca kept an eye on the windows of the gas station. This entire time they hadn't heard anything from within the store. That worried her. Going by the parked cars, there could be anywhere from two to ten people inside. And that wasn't counting how many people could've walked to the convenience store. "We need to know what's going on in there."

"Sheriff West," Stalwart was still sprawled across the console of her cruiser, "if you could grab me a fingerprint from that Kia, I can compare it to Buchanon's to get official identification. I brought all my equipment, and that includes a digital scanner."

"When he was digging through his bag, I saw him put his hand on the B pillar, the frame between the front and rear driver side doors." Hoyt pointed at the stolen vehicle.

"Viviane, get that for him."

"On it."

Sirens had been drawing closer as Rebecca spoke, and the first state trooper cruiser came into view. "Stalwart, let the troopers know what's going on. Get them to fan out and secure the area. And show them who we're looking for too. I don't want any mistakes. And for the love of all you hold dear, hold out your identification before you approach them."

Stalwart choked as she reminded him of the first time they'd met, when he'd walked onto her crime scene without identifying himself properly. She'd nearly had him tossed out on his ass.

There was no room for error this time.

Once Viviane finished lifting the print for Stalwart, with one last glance at the covered windows, Rebecca ran toward the uncovered front doors. Staying crouched while running and holding a gun wasn't easy, but that was why they practiced. Hoyt was at her back on the right with Viviane was on her left.

Sidling up to the side of the building, their formation was a near reflection of what they'd done at the bank. She prayed it wouldn't end the same way.

Hoyt broke off to take the right side of the door as

Rebecca and Viviane took the left. Before they even reached it, the sounds of wreckage reached their ears. As did the yelling voice.

Has he been doing this the whole time?

Rebecca tapped on her pen camera to record the encounter. Other than a ridiculous mess comprising all the snacks and drinks a gas station could offer, there was nothing in sight through the uncovered glass of the door. The voice was coming from behind the attendant's counter, but she couldn't see anyone back there.

"How can you fuck up something as simple as a car delivery? There was no gas in the tank! Then when I had to stop for gas, a cop, a fucking cop, pulls up next to me! You better call me back in the next few minutes, or I don't know what's going to happen."

He's in the middle of a hostage situation, and he's calling a friend for help? This isn't a game show where he can phone a friend.

She noted that Buchanon wasn't the only person on the phone. The state troopers were lined up on the street in front of the station now, with a handful of them making calls. Stalwart was also on his phone, probably updating Benson about what was happening. Even Greg, pacing the grass partition between the lot and the side road, was using his phone.

"Frost, can you see any hostages?"

"Can't see a soul, Boss." He pressed his phone against the glass and watched the screen, trying to get a better look into the building through the tinted front doors. "The racks are in my way. I can't see back to the coolers. You?"

"No customers. Buchanon's behind the counter. I don't see the attendant." Rebecca took a deep breath, running through their options. "Darby, move my cruiser out of the way and get the scoped rifle. Then get set up somewhere you'll have a good view of the counter in case we need to end this quickly."

Despite the fact that they weren't touching, Rebecca could feel Viviane go rigid at her back.

"Boss!" Hoyt's mouth gaped open as he shook his head.

"She's the best shot with a rifle and you know it, Frost." Rebecca turned to Viviane, whose complexion had gone ashen. "We've spent enough time at the range together. I know you can do this, Vi. And I need someone who's a good shot at my back. We're not getting through that mess fast or silently."

Vi's chin jerked up and then down in a stuttering nod. "Yeah, Boss."

"Wait for my order. I'll let you know when or if you should shoot. Okay?"

Still nodding, Viviane turned and ran for the cruiser parked sideways in the middle of the lot.

"She can do this, Frost." Despite her words, Rebecca wondered if she was being fair. Rhonda had noticed her tendency to show favoritism to Viviane. Though a sniper was always a good bit of insurance to have at your back, in her heart of hearts, Rebecca already felt better about the situation with Viviane moving away from the potential danger.

Hoyt chewed his lip, his gaze locked on where Viviane had disappeared behind the SUV. "Yeah, and that's the problem. This might be her first kill. I'm not ready for it." He scrubbed his hand through his hair. "I know she's not a kid, but…dammit!"

Rebecca turned back to the glass door, knowing exactly how he felt.

❋

Don't fuck up. Don't fuck up. Don't fuck up. Don't puke either. Do not make a fool of yourself here.

Viviane's stomach wriggled and squirmed like she'd drunk three strawberry milkshakes before going for a long run on the beach in the middle of August.

Dodging around the front of the sheriff's cruiser, she shoved her sidearm into her holster and snapped it secure out of long practice. The cruiser was already running to keep the battery from draining with the lights flashing. Looking at the row of state police lining up along the street, she moved the cruiser between the last two pumps and parked behind them.

With the large SUV out of the way, the troopers had a clear view of what was happening, and she was out of the way as well. She jumped out of the driver's seat and spun toward the trunk, fully aware of how much trust Rebecca was putting in her.

Her palms were covered in sweat, and she fumbled with the catch trying to open the hatchback. The wind was calm, yet she felt like it carried the contemptuous snickers of the state troopers as her fingers slid on the sun-warmed latch. It was silly, and her ears didn't perceive anything, but she simply knew they were laughing at her.

She paused and listened to her breathing instead. In. Out. The beat of her heart. In. Out.

I can do this.

Squeezing her fingers, she popped the door open. Laid flat, nestled up against the back seats, was the hardcase for the scoped rifle. It was the same one she'd used the last time she and Rebecca had gone out to practice.

In her head, she pictured herself at the long range. Sitting at the table, holding the sandbag in her left hand, the crystal-clear target off in the distance. Her mom had been taking her to the range since Viviane was only a little kid.

Back then, she'd started out on rifles because she could lie down while using them. That was long before she was strong enough to hold up a handgun, even when she used both hands. She knew every inch of the rifle, inside and out.

"It's not even a long shot. This should be easy."

The picture Hoyt had taken of Buchanon's face popped up in her mind. Once again, her stomach lurched. The technicality of the shot wasn't the problem.

It was the reality of it. Could she stare at a man through the scope of her rifle and pull the trigger, knowing he would die?

Her brain always said she could kill if it was in defense of someone else.

Her morals said it was the right thing to do if it came down to something like that.

Her bladder butted in and said she should've made a pit stop before thinking about this topic.

Her sweaty hands insisted she should not have had that last cup of coffee.

Her bladder chimed in again, agreeing with that sentiment.

She told them all to shut up and let her work.

Viviane unsnapped the hard case and lifted the rifle, coiling the sling in her left hand before gripping the stock. It was time to find a good vantage point before anyone started shooting at her friends.

34

"Call me back, Albert, you useless sack of shit!"

Though I screamed at the cell phone, it stayed deathly silent. It had full bars, and my messages were getting out, but there was no response. The landline phone dangled from where it was mounted to the wall, slowly spinning on its cord.

Peeking over the counter of the empty gas station did me no good. I'd managed to get all the blinds along the front pulled down in my temporary fortress. That had been the only tiny piece of good luck in an otherwise completely shitty situation.

How had the cops even found me? I'd changed my entire appearance. I should have been unrecognizable, a ghost.

Then that deputy in civilian clothes had rolled up. Pretending to text, but I'd caught the radio chatter. His eyes, suspicious from the get-go, had kept darting back to me. I hadn't survived this long without knowing when I was being watched.

Still, I hadn't put two and two together until I'd seen his uniform hanging in the back of his extended cab. I still couldn't believe it'd been an off-duty deputy who almost caught me.

After everything else that had gone wrong, all I could do was hole up. As soon as I'd gotten the place as secure as I could, I'd checked the back door, but it was alarmed.

Through the safety peephole, I saw that it opened into an empty lot flanked on both sides by side roads. As soon as I put a foot out that door, I'd be snatched up or shot as the emergency sirens brought all the focus on me.

And the fucking hostages that should have given me leverage? Lifting my gun, I aimed it at the metal door the clerk and customer had disappeared through. I still couldn't believe how they'd vanished like smoke before my very eyes.

Dammit. Dammit. Dammit.

With no place to go and no one to use as collateral, I was trapped. I couldn't run. I couldn't hide. I had one gun with however many bullets were left in it, my burner phone, and a useless bag full of money. Here I'd been worrying about having enough gas in the stupid car and hadn't thought to get more ammo for my gun. Shooting my way out of a situation hadn't even occurred to me.

I messaged Albert, venting about the car's empty tank. Felt good, for a second. Then more cop cars arrived. This tiny island's force, mobilizing like it was the freaking FBI.

I dropped my magazine and counted. There were only six bullets, including the one in the chamber.

What the hell? I'd only fired one shot.

The bastards from the Yacht Club hadn't even given me a full magazine.

I stared at the thick stacks of cash. Maybe I could buy my way out of here?

That wouldn't work. There were too damn many of them.

Out of options, I messaged Albert again, telling him he needed to answer me. He knew I would be on the move right now. If he had any kind of brain in his head, he'd be waiting to hear from me. Why wasn't he answering?

Gripping the phone tight in my hands, I tried to will a message to pop up. I stared at the screen. The only thing that changed was the time as the minutes ticked away.

I've been set up.

The lady back at the safe house had actually managed to save me by scaring off the Yacht Club's hit man. I knew that now.

They never planned for me to get out alive.

When that hadn't worked, they'd created this new Eliminate Hudson Plan. For me to get into a shoot-out. So the "bank robber" would be dead and no one would find out the real reason I went to that shitty-ass tiny bank.

I was a pawn this whole time.

Right now, I needed to find a smart way out of this mess they'd put me in. I screwed up by trusting them, but this whole time, they'd been giving me enough rope to hang myself.

I wasn't swinging yet.

There was only one way I was going to get out of this a free man.

Albert, what the fuck. You got me trapped.

He answered faster than he ever had before.

You shouldn't have fucked up. There are consequences for failure.

I typed the threat I had hoped I'd never have to use.

Get me out of this, or I'll turn myself in and tell them everything I know.

His reply chilled me.

Do you think the cops are with you? Or us?

35

The ranting inside had gone silent, which Rebecca hoped was a good sign. Despite feeling like she'd been there all day with the sun beating down on her, very little time had passed since the call about the stolen car.

At the familiar jingle of an officer running, Rebecca glanced over her shoulder. Deputies Jake Coffey and Trent Locke were heading for the back of the building. Two state troopers moved alongside them.

When he was even with her position, Jake called out, "Car print's positive."

Rebecca nodded a silent acknowledgement and waved him off. He ran to catch up to Locke, who'd slowed down to wait for him. They were a good team, sticking together, just as she'd instructed.

She raised her hand to turn her radio down, catching Hoyt's attention. She needed clarity, not chaos, while dealing with Buchanon. If she needed to know anything, Hoyt could pass it on to her.

"Hudson Buchanon, this is Sheriff Rebecca West. Put down your weapon and come out with your hands up."

Greg was pacing on the grassy strip, his hand waving in the air as he spoke with someone on the phone. His muffled voice was the only answer to her demands.

Testing the door, Rebecca was surprised to find it unlocked. As she nudged it open a couple inches, the sound of crinkling plastic provided evidence of Buchanon's hasty and ineffective barricade of snacks and drinks.

"No one comes in or everyone in here dies!" Buchanon's voice, youthful and tinged with fear, sliced through the stillness. He sounded like a scared kid.

Rebecca paused, her instincts on high alert. The voice was closer than expected, hidden somewhere near the counter. She had to tread carefully.

"I just want to talk, Hudson. No one needs to die today. Cooperate now, and it could mean leniency later." Rebecca let that sit for a beat. "Think about your future. You don't have to spend your whole life behind bars."

"Screw you, bitch!" Buchanon's voice cracked, and there was a quick shuffle behind the counter.

Rebecca instinctively ducked, catching Hoyt's eye. They waited, tense, for Buchanon's next move.

Hudson stayed hidden, cursing and muttering from behind the counter. Rebecca strained to listen but could only make out bits and pieces of what he was saying. A name caught her attention, though. Albert? Her mind raced. Could he be talking about Albert Gilroy of the Aqua Mafia? The same Albert who'd been a thorn in her side since the murder of his son?

Could that bastard be behind this?

With all the strange "coincidences" in this case so far, she wouldn't be surprised to find out Gilroy had been pulling the strings. This case had Aqua Mafia bullshit written all over it. But how had they gotten involved with a fairly unknown bank robber like Buchanon?

"You know, Hudson, if you want to talk about anything, now is the time." Her voice was steady despite the turmoil of her thoughts.

Rebecca caught movement out of the corner of her eye. It was Greg waving both arms at her. Once he saw he'd gotten her attention, he pointed to the phone in his hand. Then he gestured with both arms to the back of the building.

She shook her head, not understanding what he wanted. Had Locke and Jake found something?

Using his thumb and pinkie, Greg mimed holding a phone to his ear. She shook her head. She'd left hers in the cruiser. She pointed at the radio, and Greg threw up his hands in clear frustration.

We need to take a sign language course, pronto.

"I want a car," Buchanon shouted. "One with a full tank!"

Rebecca ground her teeth as Buchanon started listing his demands while Greg continued to make hand gestures that she didn't understand.

Hoyt frowned at her, and she pointed over his shoulder to where Greg stood. He clearly wasn't willing to use the radio. She mouthed, *Go talk to him.*

He nodded and ran off silently.

"That was bad luck, stealing a car on empty, huh?" She kept her tone light, feigning curiosity. She had to buy time while Hoyt learned whatever Greg was trying to tell her. It was difficult to negotiate with someone facing serious time under the best circumstances. Doing so while distracted was even harder.

"Don't make fun of me!" His voice dropped two octaves. Not like he was angry. It was more like he was trying to come across as threatening.

To Rebecca, it sounded more like a puppy trying to growl at a black bear, knowing it was pointless. But this puppy had nearly killed a man, so she couldn't let her guard down for a minute.

"I'm not making fun of you. Only asking questions. You seemed so methodical in your bank robbery. Why the oversight with the getaway car?"

Hoyt had reached Greg, and they spoke for a moment before running to the side of the building. Although she was alone at the door, she knew Viviane was following everything through her scope, watching every movement. She still had backup, but no one to check her if she screwed up this negotiation.

"It's not my fault! I didn't do that shit. Fuck! I didn't want to do any of this."

That was completely unexpected.

"Whose fault is it, then? Who did this to you?"

Her nerves were drawstring tight as she waited to hear who he blamed. Was he about to prove her gut theory right and name Albert Gilroy or the Yacht Club?

Buchanon muttered something she couldn't hear, followed by, "I'm not stupid. Making enemies is always a bad idea. And these aren't people you want as your enemy."

"I'm not sure if you've noticed it yet, Hudson. You probably can't see out too well, but you're surrounded by cops. They're all pointing guns at you. Right now, those are the enemies you need to worry about."

"But I've got hostages in here. You won't do anything to me so long as I've got them."

He had a point.

They could only see a limited area through the glass front doors. No sane cop would risk taking a shot, not knowing how many innocent bystanders were inside or where they were.

"What do you want in exchange for those hostages?" Rebecca shifted around, hoping to spot any of her deputies.

They all seemed to be taking their time at the back of the building. Without her radio on, she couldn't tell if they'd found a way in. All she could do was trust them while keeping Buchanon distracted.

"A car with a full tank. No, a van. Or an SUV. Then I want a clear path to a pier where a boat will be waiting for me. I was promised a yacht, but I'll take anything at this point. If you get me that, I'll let the hostages go." He laughed, but there was no mirth in it. "I'll even give back the money I stole from the bank. Let me get away, and you can have it all. I only want out of this."

Hoyt slunk around the corner of the building and scampered over to join her.

"What kind of boat? I don't know much about them, but I know you need different kinds and sizes depending on how many people you're taking and how long you plan on being out on the water."

Hoyt leaned forward but stopped short of the glass door. "Greg got hold of Tim Holton's mom. He's the attendant. She called Tim. They're in the back office with the door locked, safe. For now."

That explained why Greg didn't want to use the radio. Rebecca's volume was turned down, but there was still a chance Buchanon could've heard Hoyt's radio.

Smart.

"I'm going to sail far away, so I'll need a big boat to travel that far. A yacht, but one I can navigate on my own. I think that's a fair trade for the f-five p-people I got in here." Buchanon stammered a bit. He wasn't nearly as good of a liar as Rebecca was, but she gave him points for trying. It occurred to her that he might be trying to stall as much as she was.

Hoyt spoke as softly as possible. "Greg needed help breaking the window in, but he's extracting them now. Only a couple more minutes, then the staties will enter and wait for a signal."

Rebecca knew the best way to get them more time was to make Buchanon believe she was going to do whatever he wanted. That would keep him focused on the front while they cleared the store of innocent bystanders.

"That'll take a while to gas up. I'm not sure if you know this about boats or not. I learned it myself not too long ago. But even small yachts can hold hundreds of gallons of gas. That's not something you can fill up quickly. It might take an hour."

"At least two hours, Sheriff." Hoyt butted in, complicating the conversation even more to buy them the time Greg needed. "But first, we need to find someone who'll let us borrow their yacht."

Rebecca caught on to what Hoyt was thinking. "Right. Probably a dinghy, too, so that he can drop off the hostages as soon as he's safely away."

"That's right." Buchanon's voice was a mix of desperation and false bravado. "I want a clear escape."

This kid doesn't know the first thing about anything.

"I'll have my people call the marina now. Give me a few minutes." Rebecca rolled her eyes at Hoyt. It didn't matter what she said. She needed to keep talking so Buchanon stayed focused on the sound of her voice and nothing else. The best way to do that was to keep him excited about what she was offering.

"Do you do a lot of yachting, Hudson?" Rebecca wasn't sure if yachting was a verb or not.

"All the time." That sounded like a lie.

"So you know mileage and whatnot? We're not going to find you dead in the water out there, are we? I don't want to risk our hostages."

"You just...hit the gas, yeah?" He sounded like a kid in way over his head.

"I don't yacht. You're the expert here."

"Right. Expert...look, just get me something fast. And no Navy boats waiting to take me out."

"No Navy warships. I promise."

As she said the last word, Locke appeared once again. He was escorting a young man to safety. Greg and Jake were right behind him with a middle-aged man tucked between them. All five of them ran across the side street, getting as far away from the gas station as quickly as they could.

A few troopers stepped out from behind their cars, ushering them to safety. A woman with gray hair burst out of the crowd that had been forming and threw herself onto the young man.

Greg turned and gave Rebecca a big thumbs-up. She smiled. That was the kind of sign language she could absolutely understand.

But she wasn't done yet. She still had a young man she needed to get out of this situation in one piece.

So I can turn him into state's witness against the Yacht Club.

"Hey, Hudson. I've got some bad news for you." She shifted her crouch, getting ready to move if she needed to. This wouldn't make him happy, and she had to be prepared for anything.

"Let me guess. You only have sailboats available?"

She almost smiled at the whine in his voice. "No. There are all kinds of boats available. The problem is, you have nothing to trade for any of them." Rebecca kept her eyes glued on the blond hair moving on the other side of the counter. "We rescued your hostages. They're safe, and you're alone."

She paused to let that sink in.

"You're lying!"

"You know I'm not. Look, Hudson, you're surrounded with nowhere to go. You've had a rough couple of days. Come on out, and let's talk about everything that's happened."

Silence stretched for long minutes.

"Fine, but I want protection. And I want a deal."

Rebecca released a long breath. She could work with that.

"Put down your weapon, and I'll do everything in my power to make sure that happens." She meant it too.

This wasn't just about a bank robber surrendering…this was a potential goldmine of information on the Yacht Club.

The young man rose an inch at a time. Rebecca rose with him, their eyes locked over the barrel of her gun until they were both standing fully upright. He raised his empty hands, and relief surged through her every cell.

"Where's your weapon?"

He glanced at the floor. "I'm kicking it away. Don't shoot me." A second later, metal clattered against a wall.

Rebecca took several steps closer. "I won't."

Could this really be an answer to her prayers? A person willing to tell her everything he knew about the Aqua Mafia? Someone able to connect the dots and turn up the heat on the men who'd instilled fear into the residents of this island for far too long?

Would justice finally be served when Hudson Buchanon turned state's evidence against the Yacht Club? Or was that another case of wishful thinking?

36

Viviane leaned over the hood of a car in the parking lot, sweating bullets as the door to the gas station opened. Her blood pounded in her ears, and she had to remind herself to stay focused.

Relax, breathe, slow beats of the heart, focus, the same way I do on the range. Watch, wait, track.

Her hand squeezed the sandbag, and she shifted her aim as Buchanon moved along the counter toward the opening.

Rebecca had been talking to him for a bit when he'd started to stand up.

Even though his hands were in the air, that didn't mean he was unarmed.

Light danced on the surface of the glass door as it was eased open. She kept adjusting her aim. With the door open and out of the way, her shot would fly true. Passing through anything could change the trajectory of the bullet. It was always best to get a clean shot, even from a short distance.

One worry was replaced by another as she watched her boss and friend stand up too.

At the edge of the scope, Viviane could barely make out

movement, but knew it was most likely Hoyt up on the sheriff's right-hand side.

Buchanon's hands were up. His suit coat hung loosely on his frame. She couldn't tell if he had another gun on him. Viviane kept her sight centered on his chest. Rebecca would let her know one way or another if she needed to shoot.

Even though she couldn't hear any of what was happening, she watched his shirt bunch as his arms bent. His hands clasped behind his head. He was surrendering.

Adrenaline surged for a moment before she calmed herself again. It was almost over.

Only a few more minutes, and she could go at least one more day never having to kill someone. Her hand shook.

Crack!

Viviane's legs jerked with fear at the gunshot. Her arms and head held steady. Her finger immediately straightened from the trigger.

Hudson Buchanon dropped like a rock.

Her scope followed his fall before crossing over Rebecca. Her eyes were inhumanly wide in the telescopic lens as she twisted around to check behind her.

The shot hadn't come from Rebecca?

She panned to the right. Hoyt was down on one knee, twisting around. His gun slid past her position, searching for the source of the shot as well. He and Rebecca were facing the same direction.

Viviane lifted her head and turned to see what they were looking at.

There was a flurry of movement among the troopers and their cruisers. Several people were yelling. Greg's angry cursing competed with a woman's scream.

Nearly every officer had dropped to a crouch or lower, seeking cover as they searched for the shooter.

Which made it easy for Viviane to spot Trooper Dolph

Burke leaning over the roof of one of the cars with a rifle. With a pleased smirk on his face, he tapped a finger against his earpiece. Her ears were still ringing from the rush of adrenaline and her pounding heart, but she read his lips. "Shot fired. Man down."

Her skin ran hot, then cold. Rebecca didn't say to take the shot. Did she mess up? There'd been no hand gesture, no sudden movement. Nothing to indicate Buchanon was an immediate threat. His hands had been clasped behind his head, for Pete's sake.

Did Burke jump the gun? Viviane wondered if she'd missed the call somehow, if Burke had heard and acted on it instead.

No. Greg was bearing down on him, his gun pulled but not quite pointed as he barked orders at the state trooper who'd shot a man while he was surrendering. Viviane twisted her rifle around, ready to back up Greg as he approached the rogue trooper.

Burke left his rifle where it sat and raised his hands. He backed away from the weapon as Locke rushed over to grab him.

Viviane turned around to check on Rebecca and Hoyt. They were both kneeling over the unmoving body of Hudson Buchanon, bleeding on a pyre of snack cakes and energy drinks.

In the back of her head, Viviane replayed the scene in her mind. Considering how Trooper Burke had smiled after killing the man, Viviane didn't for a moment believe it had been an accident.

37

Horror warred with shock as Rebecca spun around to check on Hudson Buchanon. She couldn't see the person, but Greg and Locke had surrounded someone while yelling that they had the shooter. Trusting them to take care of that issue, she bolted toward the bleeding man.

The blow from the gunshot had knocked him onto his back, arms and legs spread wide. He'd landed on an assortment of candies and drink cans, but there was nothing close she could use to staunch the bleeding.

"Dispatch, we need medical!" Hoyt darted forward to help.

Kneeling on a box of cream-filled sponge cakes, Rebecca stared at the hole in the young man's chest. There was no need to check for a pulse. She could see it in the bubbling blood pool as it refilled before trickling down his sides.

The shot had taken Buchanon dead center.

"Medical is en route, ETA three minutes."

At the rate he was losing blood, Buchanon didn't have three minutes.

A blue roll caught Rebecca's eye. A package of shop

towels, still intact. She grabbed them, ripped the plastic wrap off, and used her entire body weight to press the roll against the wound. Blood poured out of his back from the exit wound, too, but she couldn't do much about that except press harder.

"I've got this. Go find out who fired their weapon."

Hoyt took a moment to react before getting up and running out of the store.

Buchanon's eyes were fluttering, trying to close as he stared at the ceiling.

"Can you hear me, Hudson? Blink your eyes if you can." Rebecca stared at his face, at his unmoving eyes.

Damn this entire situation! She'd had things under control. Had Viviane rushed the shot? Had she seen something through her scope that they'd missed? Did Viviane's inexperience get the better of her? His hands had been moving after she ordered him to lace his fingers behind his head. She leaned over, hoping to see a hidden weapon there, maybe tucked into his collar.

There was nothing. Leaning farther wasn't a good idea. Simply shifting her weight that little bit had let more blood leak out. She scanned the area behind him, praying to see some sign of a weapon, some reason Viviane would have had to have used lethal force.

She found nothing.

The wail of an ambulance grew loud. Rebecca craned her neck around as the echo of the siren filled the building. They'd done the same as she had, driving over the grass to park directly in front of the doors.

The woman in the passenger seat spilled out at a run, carrying a bag.

"Single gunshot wound to the chest. Unresponsive. Massive blood loss."

"Do you know his name?" The EMT dropped down

beside Rebecca, ripping open her bag. Rebecca saw the fiery red hair was secured in a tight bun at the back of her head and realized it was Anna Partridge, the same medic who'd rushed Chester Abel to the hospital in Coastal Ridge.

"Hudson Buchanon." Rebecca prepared to move out of the way as the second EMT started kicking a path through the mess to make room for the gurney.

"Mr. Buchanon, can you hear me?" Anna locked eyes with Rebecca and counted to three. At the mark, Rebecca moved away and let the professionals take over. It was eerily similar to the events that happened at Sandpiper Bank.

Had karma come full circle? Arthur Carson had managed to survive due to the quick intervention of Rebecca and Hoyt. Maybe Buchanon would be lucky too.

Rebecca stood and shuffled away from the victim to give the EMTs space to work. She glanced down at her hands. Thanks to the thick wad of shop towels, she'd managed not to get a single splatter of blood on them. Most of Buchanon's blood had rushed out the exit wound.

"Right," she said to herself, looking down. Her knees were soaked. A shower was in her near future after all.

She walked out into the sunlight.

Hoyt and Greg were approaching, both their faces screwed up as if they were sucking lemons.

"What the hell happened? He was surrendering. I didn't see any weapons." She scanned each member she could see of the two forces.

Hers were in a hodgepodge of civilian clothing and deputy vests with small marks of their profession. Viviane had the rifle slung on her back and was standing her ground, berating a trooper who seemed to be trying to get past her. The rest of the staties in their matching uniforms and department-issued sunglasses were fanned out around the man arguing with Viviane.

Jake was standing near one of the Shadow Island cruisers. The back door was open, and Rebecca could see a pair of legs in Virginia State Trooper navy blue trousers hanging out the side. Stalwart was pacing a line between the two groups.

"You're not going to believe this shit." Greg rammed his fists against his hips, twisting to glare back at the confrontation happening at the edge of the parking lot. "You remember that asshole trooper that Special Agent Lettinger chewed out a month or so ago?"

She nodded, worried where this question was leading. "Trooper Burke, yeah. I remember him. He's gunning for my job."

Greg pursed his lips as if he were about to spit but swallowed it down.

Hoyt held his hand up, motioning for Greg to wait. "Well, he's the one who gunned down Buchanon. Coffey's already relieved him of his weapons and has him sitting in the back of the car. Two of the troopers are arguing it was a good shot."

Rebecca pressed a hand to her stomach. "Do we know if Agent Lettinger is on her way?"

"According to Elliot, she's been notified and will be on her way. The troopers have already called in their captain. He's on his way down too. The rest of them are grumbling about how we're treating Burke."

"Rhonda's going to go apeshit on them." Rebecca felt a thrum of satisfaction. This was yet more proof, in her mind, that Burke was a dirty cop. "Let's go have a word with him."

Both men waited for her to take the first few steps before moving to flank her as she walked over to the gathering. The trooper, who had been up in Viviane's face, backed off as she approached.

He opened his mouth, about to say something, but she cut him off. "Do you have a problem with following standard operating procedures, Trooper..." she eyed his badge, "Moore? Because none of my people have ever had a problem handing over their guns after an officer-involved shooting."

He fidgeted but threw his shoulders back defiantly. "I—"

"Usually that gun is given to a state trooper to keep everything above board and legal." Rebecca was so mad that spittle flew her mouth, but she didn't care. "I've done it myself. Do you think Trooper Burke is above the law? Or is it that you think state troopers need to be treated with kid gloves?"

"No, Sheriff. But we're all sure it was a good shot." Moore blustered, looking over his shoulder for reinforcements. He got a few nods in response and puffed up with that assurance.

The blue wall of silence at its finest.

She gritted her teeth. "Well, considering the shot came in literally over my head and took down an unarmed suspect who was surrendering, I think maybe we should let the facts decide instead of emotions." Rebecca glanced over to where Burke was sitting.

He saw where her gaze was pointed and smirked, as stupidly cocky as he had been the last time she saw him.

"That's how things should be, Sheriff West. But there's no reason for the turf war between state and county. This is a federal crime, and the FBI has jurisdiction." Stalwart stepped up, holding his tablet in front of him like a shield.

"How the hell is a stolen car a federal crime?" A trooper named Piller, who had thus far remained quiet, stepped forward.

"When it's directly linked to an ongoing FBI investigation." Benson's voice carried well even on the tiny tablet speakers.

Stalwart turned a slow arc, letting everyone see he was on

a video conference.

"I'm Special Agent in Charge Benson. This is my case, which Sheriff West and the Shadow Island Sheriff's Office have been helping me with. I assure you that the FBI will be completely fair and diligent in their investigation into this matter and Trooper Burke's discharge of his service weapon."

That shut up the troopers and wiped the smile off Burke's face.

Rebecca remembered seeing Burke on his phone while she was talking with Buchanon, trying to get him to surrender. "I think we should also check cell phone usage. Maybe Burke was distracted while working and made a mistake."

Or maybe Burke was on a call with the same Albert who Hudson Buchanon was trying to get through to.

With the way Burke's lip started twitching, she was nearly certain they'd find matching numbers on his phone and Buchanon's.

"Deputy Frost. Secure the crime scene and the suspect's phone and weapon until the FBI forensic techs can get here. Since it was a state trooper who fired the shot, and the suspect was wanted by the FBI already, I'm sure no one will complain about that." Rebecca kept her gaze locked on Burke the whole time.

Stalwart stepped up beside her, squaring his shoulders as best he could. "I do believe you're correct, Sheriff West."

"I concur. I have a team heading your way now, and I should be there in a little more than an hour." Benson signed off.

Burke didn't look so smug anymore. Hudson Buchanon might not be able to say who paid him, but there was more than one way to get evidence.

And just like that, Rebecca had another Shadow's hoax to solve.

38

Rebecca was sitting in her SUV, keeping an eye on the Stop & Save gas station while getting updates on Arthur Carson and Hudson Buchanon. A special agent from Norfolk had driven out and taken Trooper Burke's statement along with his handgun, the rifle he used to shoot Buchanon, and his phone.

Three black SUVs parked in formation right beside the crime scene tape Hoyt and Locke had put up. The rest of her team was scattered around the building, protecting pieces of evidence.

Benson was the first person out, and he waved a hand, indicating for his people to get started while he walked over to Rebecca. He buttoned his suit jacket while glaring around the area, taking everything in. FBI agents and deputies turned and quickly got back to work under that gaze. "Break it down for me, West. What the hell is going on out here?"

His expression was fierce, but Rebecca was used to that. She turned and pointed toward the store. "Our bank robber found someplace to lay low until this afternoon."

"And...?"

She twisted to the side and indicated the direction of the

beach parking lot. "Then he stole a car from a public beach. He was spotted in the act by someone who was able to not only give a detailed description of the car, including a complete license plate number, but who also described him down to his accessories."

Benson's expression was a blank mask. "Really?"

Turning back to the front, she gestured with both hands. "Deputy Frost spotted the vehicle and followed it. Buchanon identified Frost, ran inside, and failed to take hostages. I overheard him making a phone call, demanding help to get him out of this. It might have been a man named Albert. I'm not sure."

Benson waved a hand. "Go on."

Some stray hairs fell into her face, and she tucked them behind her ear. "After we got the hostages out of the building, Buchanon readily surrendered. While he was following every order, Virginia State Trooper Dolph Burke took a shot over the heads of Frost and me, striking Buchanon in the chest. This occurred conveniently after Buchanon explained that some men had hired him to rob the bank and he was willing to give them up for a lighter sentence."

Benson's stoic expression cracked. His right eyebrow darted upward briefly, but for him it was quite a tell. "He was hired to rob the bank?"

"That's what his new burner phone implies." Rebecca gazed across the parking lot into the store. She stared at the cleared section of the floor where the pool of blood was rimmed with convenience food chaos. "I'm so glad you get to deal with the majority of this paperwork."

Benson glowered, but she ignored it, confident that she was as funny as she thought. And she had a damn good reason for her remarks.

"This is going to require federal levels of investigation. I know how to do it, but even with my extended budget, there's no way I could do justice to this case with my handful of deputies."

With a grunt of agreement, Benson nodded. "Okay, now that you've walked me through the general problems of this case, take me through what happened this afternoon. Step by step."

Rebecca's phone rang, and she glanced at the screen. "Hold up. This is my people calling back with an update on the anonymous tip about the stolen car." She answered the phone and put it on speakerphone. "Elliot, you're on with SAC Benson and me. What did you find?"

"Hi, Sheriff West, it's Melody too. Elliot couldn't figure out how to get all the information you needed, and I was coming on shift anyway, so I'm helping him out."

Benson sidled closer, and Rebecca lifted the phone so it would be easier for him to hear. "All I need to know right now is if there's any ID for the phone used to make that report."

"There is, but it's a carrier's account, not assigned to any individual we can find yet." Elliot's answer was crisp and precise. And not at all helpful.

"You spoke to her. Is there anything else you remember hearing? Anything in the background? Did she have an accent?"

"Not any accent that stands out around here. No, ma'am. It was an older woman, though. And I could hear the ocean behind her. Not only the wind but waves crashing as well. It sounded like she was on a beach, not an ocean or the pier. There wasn't that staccato crashing that happens with things in the water."

Rebecca was amazed at his ability to discern the difference in sound from waves striking a beach instead of a synthetic object. It was one of the things people must pick up from living in one area for so long. The same way people in the country could pick out different bird calls. "Good. Anything else? Can you play me the recorded message?"

"I can't. The caller didn't use the nine-one-one line. She called a station phone."

That was weird.

"Okay. Then close your eyes and see if it helps you remember."

"Yeah. Yeah. It was weird. The way she was talking. It sounded more like she was reading off a list when she described the car. That didn't seem unusual at the time, since most people don't have that information memorized, even for their own cars. Oh, but she sounded natural when describing the man, as if she was describing someone standing in front of her."

Melody butted in. "We already tried calling the number back, but the phone seems to be turned off because it goes straight to an unregistered voicemail. Also, I looked up the car, just because I find that's a good way to get extra information for you guys. I found a BOLO for it from this morning."

Elliot jumped back in, almost like they were fighting to see who could give the most information. A trait Rebecca appreciated in nearly everyone she worked with. "It was reported stolen this morning from a residence in Coastal Ridge."

"So it was stolen twice?" Rebecca lifted her gaze to Benson.

"But the caller said it was being stolen at the time of the call this afternoon. That's weird, right?"

"Very weird." Benson shifted, looking at the stolen car and the wrecked gas station. "Can you send us the information about who filed that report this morning?"

"Yes, sir. We'll send it over as soon as we get it." Melody sounded excited as she ended the call.

"I think you might be right. This is going to need to be a forensically heavy case if we're going to find Hudson Buchanon's coconspirators."

Rebecca tucked her phone into her pocket. "He's still alive. We might be able to get a confession out of him anyway. He did not seem eager to go to jail. But he was willing to turn himself in. Oh, and make sure you take a lot of pictures and get copies of anything you can."

"Are you hiding something from me?" Benson focused on her face, waiting for her to give away her thoughts.

"Lot of things." Rebecca nodded. "Tons of things, really."

"Then why don't you go ahead and tell me?"

"Because even outside, the walls in Shadow Island all seem to have ears." She gestured around at the mostly empty streets and the few locals who were watching from inside other buildings or from their cars.

"So you're not keeping quiet because crime has skyrocketed since you got here."

Rebecca knew that one day, likely in the very near future, she'd need federal help to take down the Aqua Mafia and all their stooges. "It might have something to do with that, too, yeah. Tell you what, it's a long story. And it would make more sense with the paperwork that goes with it."

A fourth black SUV pulled up, and forensic techs started spilling out.

"Just tell me when and where. You don't have to do this alone, Rebecca."

She tried to smile, but her lips wouldn't obey. "I'll even go back to the office and start putting things together for you. It's going to be a slog to get through it all. I spent all summer trying to do that myself."

"Rebecca," Benson leaned in, "what have you gotten

yourself into on this island?" He nodded toward the pen in her pocket. "And why are you resorting to these instead of basic body cams?"

"I don't know, Percy. So many times, I keep thinking I'm paranoid, only to learn I wasn't wary enough. But maybe you can help me figure it all out." She waved for her deputies to come join her so the crime scene could be handed over. "Meet me at the station once you're done, and we can go over everything."

39

Rebecca was sorting stacks of paperwork in her office when a knock on the door caught her attention. It was first thing in the morning, but she'd already been in for hours and was on her fourth cup of coffee. Normally, her door was open, so no one ever bothered her when they saw that it was closed.

Which meant it could only be one person out there knocking. Quickly, she made sure that all the piles were laid properly. "Come in."

The door swung open, and Benson stepped inside.

"Okay, you've dragged this out long enough, Sheriff West. Explain what's going on in your little town that would lead to a man being paid to rob a bank."

She waved toward a chair. "Have a seat."

Benson closed the door before dropping into a chair and resting his ankle on his opposite knee. "Thanks to your dire warning yesterday, I had my people work all through the night, triple-checking everything, and even going back to double-check the evidence from the bank and the Longfellow property. We still haven't located him, by the way. I'm beginning to think your paranoia is contagious."

Rebecca tried not to let those words hurt her. After all, she'd been the one to bring up the bit about paranoia yesterday. "I also said it's complicated." She patted the tops of paper stacks on her desk. "And I meant it."

He raised an eyebrow. "What's all this about?" He leaned forward, then froze. "This had better not be a prank and all these papers are blank."

"No. They're not." She frowned and eyed the stacks. "But that would've been a good one. I'll have to remember that for later. This is sadly all too real and impacts nearly every family that lives on this island. Let's start with the most recent cases. Did you hear about the oversight investigation the VSP started on me and Shadow Island's recent crime wave?"

Benson's other eyebrow lifted to join the first near his hair line. "No. But it has to be serious if there was an investigation into it."

"It was. And it wasn't. You see, for the forty previous years before I became sheriff, there was nearly no crime reported on this island. A few drug deals. Boating accidents. Drunk-and-disorderly charges. And the usual complaints about unpaid tabs and things like that."

He nodded. "That sounds unrealistically idyllic."

"Doesn't it?" Rebecca picked up her coffee. "Then Sheriff Alden Wallace died, and I took over. And I found all this."

"Which you still haven't explained to me." Benson's foot bounced.

"It's the last twenty-ish years' worth of crimes that were never properly investigated, let alone filed with the courts."

Benson froze, staring at the dozen or so foot-tall piles. "Unfiled?"

"Yeah, and these are the weird ones. We've got bodies found floating. People gone missing. Houses broken into. All kinds of drug charges. Unlawful possession of a pet alligator.

That's one of my favorites. An obscene amount of reckless driving, speeding, racing, and drunk driving charges." Rebecca took a sip of her coffee as Benson leaned forward and started flipping through the paperwork.

"Dear god."

"Solicitation of a minor. Improper handling of alcohol, tobacco, *and* firearms. So many Mann Act violations I haven't bothered to count them all. Improper handling of human remains. Fraud. Blackmail. Most of them are small- to mid-range criminals, but they're being bailed out on cash bonds by senators' sons. They have high-priced lawyers like Shania Lynch and Braden Schaefer, who are known to defend mobsters."

"If there's so many, why weren't they filed? And why do you have them now?" Benson's voice was low, with a hint of warning in it. "These are serious charges, Rebecca."

"Because they're not mine, and I'm still digging them up and sorting through them. This was all left to me by my predecessor. None of it was filed by date or even type of crime. As far as I was able to figure out, they were filed by connections, originally."

"Why?"

Rebecca shook her head. "Like the first one I read was a drug dealer charged with possession and intent to sell. The next one was a drunk driving. The one after that was a noise complaint. What did they have in common? The same man bailed all of them out."

Benson opened another folder. "Interesting."

Leaning back in her chair, she kept her eyes locked onto Benson's. "This is literal decades of organized crime showing a sheriff who lost hope in the system when he noticed the same problems happening over and over again when they got to court. Tossed out on technicalities. Improper handling of evidence. Missing evidence. Witnesses not showing up."

"This report is about Luka Reynold." Benson tapped a folder. "Isn't that the son of one of the lobbyists in D.C.?"

"And now you see how a small-town sheriff might've found himself in over his head with even the smallest cases when people like the Reynold family are the ones bailing them out and buying them lawyers. And when all those people are constant visitors to the same marina here, along with senators, news anchors, and district attorneys from up and down the coast, I'm sure you can see where this is going."

He ran a hand down his face. "Yes…I see it."

She waved her hands in frustration. "Shit, Benson, name a powerful position, and we've got one of them in these files. And all of them are either members or guests of the Yacht Club. Mitchell Longfellow was a proud member of the Yacht Club, and I believe Richmond Vale, the Select Board head, is connected to them in some way as well."

Rebecca pushed her chair back and bumped into the bookcase behind her desk. "Anyone who has a slip at the marina is a member. But I still don't understand their hierarchy. It might be based on personal wealth, since the younger ones seem to be a step below the older men, but they're still above some of the people that don't have yachts at the Seaview."

"The Yacht Club?"

"Yeah, it sounds like a kid's club. But that's really what they call themselves. We call them the Aqua Mafia now." She smirked and shook her head. "And they know how to do a lot of underhanded crap. Enough so that it affected nearly everyone in this office until they offered the late Sheriff Wallace a truce. He would look the other way when certain names came up on reports, and they would stop destroying the lives of the people he cared about."

"What about you?" Benson waved the report with Luka's name on it at her. "Did they ever offer you a truce?"

Rebecca grinned, showing all her teeth. "Not even once. They've threatened me a lot, though. Who do you think is behind the man trying to buy my rental house out from under me?"

"But why wouldn't they offer you the same deal they offered Wallace?" He crossed his arms.

She shrugged and ducked her head. "Maybe because the first case on Shadow Island that I worked on, I went directly for their throats. I arrested two out of three of their men that night. Locke shot two of them, and the one I brought down pled guilty. I guess he wasn't important enough to get the high-priced lawyer. The third, the one who actually pulled the trigger and killed Wallace, survived being shot and is still getting extensions for his court date."

"This sounds a lot like why you left the FBI in the first place."

Rebecca had been worried about that. It didn't matter that she'd been right when she'd gone hunting down lobbyists and senators the first time. It was political suicide. At least, the way she'd gone about it was. Hopefully, Benson would have better discretion and resources than she'd had back then.

"Maybe it does. Maybe you think I'm seeing conspiracies where there are none. But look at those reports. Read all the reports Special Agent Rhonda Lettinger with the GIS has done. Check into the cases she's worked down here. One of their other victims was a sitting senator. You'll have to talk to the special agent in charge in D.C. to hear about that, though. It wasn't one of my cases, only linked to one of mine."

Benson stared at her, not giving anything away. "The problem with all this, Rebecca, is there's no federal case these can piggyback on. It's all local crimes, most of them small. I don't have any jurisdiction in crimes like this."

"Which is why Wallace was doing his best to set up a RICO investigation. And I've continued with that work. That *is* your jurisdiction. I've added my case files and notes for the ones I've gotten since becoming sheriff here."

"I was wondering where you were going with this." Benson sat forward, replacing the paper he'd picked up. "Okay, I can have Stalwart delve into all these cases. Do you have a box I can put them in?"

Rebecca inclined her head to the boxes stacked against the wall. "I did. But I used them all on the copies I made for you. These are only the ones that didn't fit." She patted the papers still on her desk.

"Dammit, this had better not be a prank." He got up and tried to bat away the top box. It didn't move since it was filled to the brim with papers. Definitely not a prop.

"It's no prank. This is deadly serious. They're already trying to get rid of us, any way they can. I've also included a copy of my personal medical records. You can see what they've already done to me. As soon as they find out about the FBI hauling fifteen cases of papers out of here, they're going to start gunning for me even harder. And I won't back down."

This was the part Rebecca had been trying not to think about when she'd decided it was time to reach out for help.

"Remember what I said about evidence going missing." She handed him three flash drives. "These are the digital backups for everything. In case I do end up dead, the name of my killer will most likely be in one of those files."

Benson stared at Rebecca for a long while, then finally nodded and took the drives. "I'll have Stalwart go through everything. If he thinks it's solid enough to pursue, I'll put together a task force."

That was better than she'd hoped for. And if Benson

could get through the red tape fast enough, he might be able to put a stop to the Yacht Club before they managed to kill her.

40

Rebecca finished writing the email to Agent Stalwart on her work computer. The door to her office was closed, but the air was still thick with dust and paint fumes as the final touches of the remodel were completed. Having the door closed was the only way she could escape the din so she could think. Pressing the send button, she hoped the answers she'd given for Stalwart's many questions would help move the case along.

In the two weeks since Benson had taken away the copies of Wallace's files, there hadn't been so much as a whisper that the Yacht Club even knew about what she'd done. She hadn't dared to think about it until Benson had called her up a few days ago to let her know that he was assembling a task force to deal with it.

That night, she'd toasted her triumph with Ryker and Humphrey on the back porch of her rental. She'd spent all night discussing the implications with him. He'd been worried for her safety at first and what it could mean for her reelection chances, so she'd downplayed how quickly a task force could see results.

The latest bit of work finished, she got up from her desk, picked up her empty mug, and opened the door…where she was met with a chubby, denim-covered backside.

"Oh, sorry, Sheriff. I was just finishing up the trim here." Larry the handyman picked up his tools and shuffled out of her way.

Rebecca peeked around him. The area that had once been their unofficial lounge room was now divided in half by a set of heavy-duty bars. They'd managed to fit two cells into the room.

The couch had already been moved to the empty room near the back door. Hoyt had insisted on keeping it so they'd have some place to nap. Considering how many times she'd already used it for that, she didn't argue.

"Looks good, Larry. Were you able to figure out how to set the key card reader into the wall and get it to work?" She pointed to the still empty cutout in the wall next to her office door.

"I did. Yeah. Had to call the manufacturer to be sure. I'll get that put together after the paint dries and I can put the new door up."

She was glad she'd thought to add that feature. It was about time the station was brought into the 1990s, at least. The short hallway that led to the room would have two of the readers, one for the holding cell area and another for the interrogation room. A third would be added to the locker room for added security. Each required both a card and a personal passcode.

"By the way, the kitchenette is all done. Hoyt brewed some coffee too." Larry laughed as she perked up.

"Then I guess it's about time I took it for a test drive." Rebecca didn't run for the bullpen, but she did speed walk.

The old, rickety table they'd been using for their drink station was gone. So was the floating sink. In their place was a basic countertop in the corner of the room. It had an inset sink, two cabinets, and three drawers. The coffee maker was the same, but it looked much better on a solid, shiny, cream-colored laminate surface. Rebecca had even splurged and gotten them a mini-fridge that fit in right beside the counter.

"There's the lady I was hoping to see." Hoyt waved.

She scowled at him. "What is it, Frost? Don't tell me another building has gotten vandalized."

Lately, they'd been having a problem with homes and businesses getting spray-painted. Hoyt insisted it was merely a bunch of island boys getting bored now that school had been in full swing for a few months and the pretty tourist girls had stopped coming down to sunbathe on the beaches in the chilly weather.

"I wish. Sadly, we got a call about a possible abduction, but it could also be an assault."

Rebecca slowed on her way to pouring her first cup of coffee in her new break area. "There's a big difference between the two."

"Yeah, Boss." He held out a report form for her to read. "But all we have is a pool of blood, a single witness who isn't clear on what she saw, and no victim in sight."

Rebecca took the report and scanned it. Then she looked up at Hoyt and offered a tired smile. "It's never easy, is it? We can never have the bad guy standing with the gun in his hand and smoke still pouring from the barrel."

"The easy ones just aren't our style, Sheriff."

The End
To be continued...

Thank you for reading.
All of the Shadow Island books can be found on Amazon.

ACKNOWLEDGMENTS

How does one adequately express gratitude to all those who have transformed a shared dream into a stunning reality? Let us attempt to do just that.

First and foremost, our families deserve our deepest thanks. Their unwavering support and encouragement have been our bedrock, allowing us the time and energy to translate our collective imagination into the words that fill these pages. Their belief in our vision has been a constant source of strength and inspiration.

As coauthors, our journey has been uniquely collaborative and rewarding. Now, with Mary also embracing the additional role of publisher, our adventure has taken on an exciting new dimension. This transition from solely writing to also publishing has been both a challenge and a joy, opening doors to share our work more directly with you, our readers.

We are immensely grateful to the entire team at Mary Stone Publishing — a group who believed in our potential from the very beginning. Their commitment extends beyond editing our words; it encompasses the tireless efforts of designers, marketers, and support staff, all dedicated to bringing our stories to life. Their expertise, creativity, and passion have been vital in capturing the essence of our tales and sharing them with the world.

However, our greatest appreciation is reserved for you, our beloved readers. You took a chance on our book, generously sharing your most precious asset—your time. It is our fervent hope that the pages of this book have rewarded that generosity, offering you a journey worth taking and memories that linger.

With all our love and heartfelt appreciation,

Mary & Lori

ABOUT THE AUTHOR

Nestled in the serene Blue Ridge Mountains of East Tennessee, Mary Stone crafts her stories surrounded by the natural beauty that inspires her. What was once a home filled with the lively energy of her sons has now become a peaceful writer's retreat, shared with cherished pets and the vivid characters of her imagination.

As her sons grew and welcomed wonderful daughters-in-law into the family, Mary's life entered a quieter phase, rich with opportunities for deep creative focus. In this tranquil environment, she weaves tales of courage, resilience, and intrigue, each story a testament to her evolving journey as a writer.

From childhood fears of shadowy figures under the bed to a profound understanding of humanity's real-life villains, Mary's style has been shaped by the realization that the most complex antagonists often hide in plain sight. Her writing is characterized by strong, multifaceted heroines who defy traditional roles, standing as equals among their peers in a world of suspense and danger.

Mary's career has blossomed from being a solitary author to establishing her own publishing house—a significant milestone that marks her growth in the literary world. This expansion is not just a personal achievement but a reflection of her commitment to bring thrilling and thought-provoking stories to a wider audience. As an author and publisher, Mary continues to challenge the conventions of the thriller genre, inviting readers into gripping tales filled with serial killers, astute FBI agents, and intrepid heroines who confront peril with unflinching bravery.

Each new story from Mary's pen—or her publishing house—is a pledge to captivate, thrill, and inspire, continuing the legacy of the imaginative little girl who once found wonder and mystery in the shadows.

Discover more about Mary Stone on her website.
www.authormarystone.com

Lori Rhodes

As a tiny girl, from the moment Lori Rhodes first dipped her toe into the surf on a barrier island of Virginia, she was in love. When she grew up and learned all the deep, dark secrets and horrible acts people could commit against each other, she couldn't stop the stories from coming out of the other end of her pen. Somehow, her magical island and the darkness got mixed together and ended up in her first novel. Now, she spends her days making sure the guests at her beach rental cottages are happy, and her nights dreaming up the characters who love her island as much as she does.

Connect with Mary online

facebook.com/authormarystone
x.com/MaryStoneAuthor
goodreads.com/AuthorMaryStone
bookbub.com/profile/3378576590
pinterest.com/MaryStoneAuthor
instagram.com/marystoneauthor
tiktok.com/@authormarystone

Made in the USA
Middletown, DE
20 November 2024